"This would be for you, Becca."

"Right. We've got two weeks and I've got stitches and a gimpy arm. I'm sure that inspires a lot of lust in you."

He continued to stare at her, not speaking.

Criminy, he really was serious.

She'd been consumed with the thought of having a baby for months, maybe even years, and had usually cast Colby in the starring "sperm donor" role. But that had been fantasy, not real life.

She leaped up from the sofa, slid her feet into her shoes. "I need to go open the store."

He nodded and stood, surprising her when he let the subject drop.

Lord have mercy. Now, as seven years ago, there was a deal on the table.

And by dog, she was really tempted to take it.

Dear Reader,

I love small towns and close-knit communities and anything Southern. Probably because I'm a Southerner by birth, who's been transplanted to California.

Tempted by a Texan—Becca Sue's book—is the final book in my TEXAS SWEETHEARTS series. I want you all to know that I truly appreciate the letters and e-mails you've sent asking for Becca's book, and the wonderful, uplifting comments you've given me along the way.

I believe in second chances and that with age and maturity people can see one another in a different light. That's the case with Becca Sue and Colby Flynn. They were soul mates when they were young, but didn't realize it until life and several years had passed, showing them what could have been…and what can always be.

I hope you enjoy Becca and Colby's journey as they are both tempted, once again, to reach for happily-ever-after, as they learn to bend and compromise and let love take its true and rightful course.

I love to hear from readers. You can e-mail me at mindyneff@aol.com, or through my Web site at www.mindyneff.com.

All my best,

Mindy Neff

Tempted by a Texan

MINDY NEFF

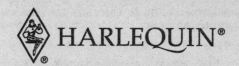

HARLEQUIN®

TORONTO • NEW YORK • LONDON
AMSTERDAM • PARIS • SYDNEY • HAMBURG
STOCKHOLM • ATHENS • TOKYO • MILAN • MADRID
PRAGUE • WARSAW • BUDAPEST • AUCKLAND

ISBN-13: 978-0-373-75146-4
ISBN-10:   0-373-75146-X

TEMPTED BY A TEXAN

This edition published by arrangement with Harlequin Books S.A.

® and TM are trademarks of the publisher. Trademarks indicated with ® are registered in the United States Patent and Trademark Office, the Canadian Trade Marks Office and in other countries.

www.eHarlequin.com

Printed in U.S.A.

ABOUT THE AUTHOR

Mindy Neff published her first book with Harlequin American Romance in 1995. Since then, she has appeared regularly on the Waldenbooks bestseller list and won numerous awards, including the National Readers' Choice award, the *Romantic Times BOOKclub* Career Achievement award and three W.I.S.H. awards for outstanding hero. She has also been nominated twice for the prestigious RITA® Award.

Originally from Louisiana, Mindy settled in Southern California, where she married a really romantic guy and raised five kids. Family, friends, reading, grandkids and a very spoiled Maltese named Harley are her passions.

Books by Mindy Neff

HARLEQUIN AMERICAN ROMANCE

857—THE SECRETARY GETS HER MAN
898—CHEYENNE'S LADY
906—PREACHER'S IN-NAME-ONLY WIFE
925—IN THE ENEMY'S EMBRACE
946—THE INCONVENIENTLY ENGAGED PRINCE
993—COURTED BY A COWBOY*
998—SURPRISED BY A BABY*
1001—RESCUED BY A RANCHER*

*Texas Sweethearts

Don't miss any of our special offers. Write to us at the following address for information on our newest releases.

Harlequin Reader Service
U.S.: 3010 Walden Ave., P.O. Box 1325, Buffalo, NY 14269
Canadian: P.O. Box 609, Fort Erie, Ont. L2A 5X3

To Shari and Stephen. It took you almost eleven years to realize you were soul mates. Just goes to show that your love was meant to be. I love you both!

And to Elektra Skye—our little miracle. You are so perfect and so loved. Tell Mommy that Nana wants more grandbabies.

Chapter One

Becca Sue Ellsworth's arms felt empty. It was an ache that went clear to her soul.

From her apartment window above her bookshop and antiques boutique, Becca's Attic, she gazed out at Main Street, darkened now except for streetlamps casting shadowy arcs over the two-lane road. There was no traffic. The diagonal parking spaces in front of the sidewalks were deserted. Hope Valley was one of those small Southern towns that rolled up the sidewalks at dusk.

A deep sense of aloneness pressed against her chest. She'd just spent the evening with her three best friends—more affectionately known as the Texas Sweethearts—and their families. She wasn't normally given to envy, and it made her feel small to covet her girlfriends' children, pregnancies and happy families.

Oh, it wasn't as though she begrudged them their happiness. She just wanted a piece of it for herself.

Younger by six months than Sunny, Donetta and

Tracy Lynn, Becca had recently celebrated her thirtieth birthday. The magic number, it seemed, when a woman's biological clock began to gong like a cowbell being beaten by a sledgehammer.

The incessant reminder was almost deafening.

She didn't have the money for artificial insemination, which Tracy Lynn had tried. And she didn't have a husband like Sunny and Donetta—and, of course, Tracy Lynn. Tracy Lynn had practically been forced into a marriage of convenience, which had ultimately turned out to be her heart's every dream come true.

Sighing, Becca looked past her own reflection in the window and caught a glimpse of movement below. Her heart jumped into her throat, and with a silent yelp, she quickly ducked behind the silky Priscilla curtains.

Colby Flynn.

The streetlight illuminated him as he walked down the sidewalk and paused outside his law office, which was right across the street from Becca's Attic. He started to insert the key, then turned suddenly, looking directly up at Becca's window.

She hit the wall beside the window with a thud, flattening her back against the blue forget-me-nots speckled across the antique wallpaper, and held her breath. It was a wonder she hadn't wet her pants.

That was all she needed—to get caught staring at her ex-boyfriend.

Lord, the man could still make her heart bump against her ribs. More so lately. And all because of a silly promise made when they were both drunk on their butts.

Shoot, he probably didn't even remember. It'd been seven years.

They'd dated, even tried living together for a couple of months one summer when Colby took a semester off from law school, but they'd soon found out that they were total opposites who drove each other nuts. She'd been a scatterbrained free spirit. He'd been a neatnik, stuffy sort who hadn't appreciated the fact that clothes lying about on the floor was an excellent way to preserve the life of the carpet.

Maybe she'd scared him off. At twenty-three, she'd been going through her I-want-to-get-married-and-have-babies phase. Colby was set on building a future in the field of law, not housekeeping. He'd told her he couldn't give her what she wanted, that he had to let her go so she could find someone else who could fulfill her dream, give her the things she deserved—commitment and family.

Even now a wave of embarrassment washed over her as she recalled the pitiful plea in her voice: "What if that doesn't happen? I'm all that's left of my family, Colby. What if I turn thirty someday and haven't found my soul mate?"

"You *will* turn thirty," he'd teased. "And I'm sure a smarter man than me will have snapped you up way sooner than that."

"But what if?" she'd persisted.

"Then we'll have a baby together," he'd said, wiping the tears from her face, her alcohol-induced misery clearly too much for him to resist. "No strings attached. You'll have your family, I'll take care of the finances."

Well, her birthday had already passed. And because Colby's office was right across the street from her shop and apartment, she was hyperaware of his comings and goings.

Every time it looked as though he might make the trek across the street, an adrenaline surge nearly knocked her to her knees.

Did he remember?

Neither of them had ever mentioned the words they'd said to each other seven years ago, words that made sense in the midst of an alcoholic haze, but could only be deemed ridiculous in the sober light of day.

Several times lately, though, when their paths crossed, Colby had given her a teasing, flirtatious wink and a knowing look.

What was up with that? And what in the world did it mean?

She was becoming a wreck obsessing over it, probably because of the trips she'd been making to the hospital's maternity ward lately.

First Donetta and Storm Carmichael—they'd had a beautiful baby girl. Tracy Lynn and Linc Slade were next—another precious baby girl. And Sunny Carmichael-Slade was due to deliver any day now— the sonogram showed it was a boy.

Gathering her nerve, Becca carefully inched to the side and sneaked a peek out the window. Colby was no longer on the sidewalk and a light inside his office indicated he'd gone in.

Both relief and disappointment washed over her. *Criminy, Becca Sue. Get a grip.*

Most likely, she was merely projecting her own wishes onto Colby—thinking his overt glances in her direction carried undertones of their youthful baby pact.

Annoyed with herself at the silliness, she crossed the room, climbed into bed and snatched up a knitting magazine from her nightstand.

Neither she nor Colby would consider hopping in the sack just to produce a child and then go on their respective ways.

Besides, Colby Flynn had broken her heart. Oh, sure, she'd made a point of *not* letting him know that. She'd been determined to act sophisticated, to play off their breakup as no big deal, insisting they continue their friendship—which they had, albeit as slightly distant friends.

Sadly, she would never easily trust a man with her heart again.

Especially Colby Flynn.

She flipped through the pages of the knitting magazine. It was the fall edition and she couldn't work up much enthusiasm for trendy hat-and-sweater patterns when the temperature outside this week had barely made it below seventy degrees. In Becca's opinion, it was silly to send out the fall issue of a publication in the middle of June.

After a few more minutes, she set aside the magazine and turned out the light. As her eyes adjusted to the dark, the barely perceptible smell of animals from the area's horse and cattle ranches wafted in the gentle breeze, shifted the gauzy curtains at her window, and mingled with the lemon verbena scent of her linens. What would probably seem like an odd combination of odors to others was actually comforting to Becca Sue. With every breath, she felt wrapped in a sense of the familiar, in generational roots that went as far back as the defenders of the Alamo.

What was Colby doing at his office so late at night? she wondered. Darla Pam Kirkwell, Hope Valley's self-appointed busybody, had mentioned that she'd heard he was leaving town, but then, Darla Pam loved to gossip and stir up trouble and her information was not always reliable.

Becca gave a start when she heard a noise coming from downstairs. A crash.

"Darn it, Trouble!" She threw back the bedsheet and got up. The silly cat was always getting into something he shouldn't. Trouble lived up to his name nicely—although Becca should have tacked on the middle name of Klepto. Over the past few months, her cat had actually been *stealing* things from the neighbors! Shiny hair clips from Donetta's salon, spoons from Anna's café, trinkets from the hardware store and saddle shop…it was starting to get embarrassing.

The cat was either going to get arrested or Becca would have to take her to a shrink. Perhaps she ought to rethink the kitty doors she'd installed. Clearly the little menace needed less freedom.

"I swear, Trouble, if you've broken any of my prize collectibles, I'll take you to jail myself."

Without bothering to put on a robe, Becca opened the door at the top of the steep staircase that led to her shop below and flicked on the light switch. The single, low-wattage bulb didn't even have the courtesy to give a pop to let her know it was burned out. It simply didn't come on.

No problem. She knew the layout of the building by heart, right down to the last creaky board, and she always kept a flashlight behind the cash register in case of major storms or power outages.

Besides, she was all too aware that Colby was right across the street, and since she rarely pulled the shades over the front windows, she didn't particularly want to turn on the store lights. That would make Becca's Attic the equivalent of a lighted aquarium, and Becca the parading fish.

Her bare feet made only a whisper of sound on the wood treads. She counted thirteen steps, then reached for the crystal knob she knew was right in front of her on the door at the bottom of the stairs.

She expected the shrill of squeaky hinges.

She did *not* expect the blinding pain when something slammed into her side.

Or the next blow that buckled her knees.

COLBY FLYNN sealed another carton of law books and carried it to the growing stack piled neatly by the front door. He still had three weeks before he was scheduled to relocate to Dallas, but there was a lot of packing to do. He hadn't realized how much stuff he'd accumulated since he'd been back in Hope Valley.

He also hadn't realized how stupidly melancholy he'd feel about leaving his hometown and friends.

He touched the corkboard hanging on the wall by the front entrance. It was overflowing with lawyer jokes, some written on pieces of scrap paper, all of them held in place by colorful pushpins. Nearly everyone who crossed this threshold and saw the wall art ended up coming back and pinning their own joke to the board. Over the years, the collection had become vast.

This was his one and only concession to clutter.

Granted, he'd tried organizing the contents of the corkboard in the beginning, but it had been a losing battle. So he'd given in and let his friends have their fun—a difficult concession for a guy who'd attended military school and had organization burned into his brain.

Although some of the paper was yellowed with age and the board looked like a scrap hoarder's mess, Colby hated to part with the thing.

But this wasn't the sort of art appropriate for the tastefully elegant walls of the Wells and Steadman law firm, soon to be Wells, Steadman and Flynn.

Leaving the corkboard where it was for the time being, he pushed the stack of packing boxes against the baseboard and turned to see what else needed doing. A flash of light caught his eye and he paused.

For a minute he thought his tired eyes were

playing tricks on him. He could have sworn he saw a beam of light coming from Becca's shop, which had been dark for quite a while now. Her upstairs apartment lights had switched off almost an hour ago—yes, damn it, he reminded himself, he'd noticed.

Moving his law practice to the building across from Becca's Attic last year had been both heaven and torture. Heaven because he got to see Becca's cute little body sashaying in and out day after day.

And torture because he had to watch her cute little body sashaying in and out day after day—knowing he'd tossed away any chance of actually touching or holding her.

Although his regret was deep, he still believed that he'd done the right thing seven years ago by letting her go. She was a woman who deserved commitment, steadiness and roots.

Because of his family's track record, those were the things in life he feared most—along with failure.

The narrow beam glanced off the darkened window again. Why would Becca be prowling around with a flashlight at midnight? Why not just turn on the lights?

He didn't like the suspicions that came to mind. Curse of the profession—he'd been privy to way too many cases involving crimes where people stole from others because they were too damn lazy to go out and make their own money; or they were such slaves to drugs that their jobs weren't enough to fund their habit and they had to take what didn't belong to them.

Well, by God, nobody was going to steal from Becca Sue. Not if he had anything to say about it.

He removed a Colt .45 handgun from the file cabinet and stuffed it in the waistband of his jeans at the small of his back. Leaving his office, he sprinted across the street and slipped into the alley that led to the back entrance.

The door to her shop was ajar.

His heart lodged right up under his Adam's apple and his mouth went dry. He slid the Colt from his jeans and checked the safety.

Using his knuckles so he wouldn't sully any potentially incriminating fingerprints with his own, he eased the door open the rest of the way and crept inside, taking a moment to let his eyes adjust to the darkness.

Nothing moved. No sound.

He could hear his own breath loudly in his ears. A sixth sense told him he wasn't alone.

Simultaneously, he heard a moan and the sound of a car engine roaring to life. The moan was female and coming from inside. The pitch of the vehicle's muffler indicated it was accelerating away. Fast.

He slammed his hand against the wall, groping in the dark for the light switch. The side of his palm brushed the toggle and fluorescent lights blinked on, illuminating half the store.

Oh, man. Becca lay in a crumpled heap just beyond the stairwell doorway.

Chapter Two

Colby swore, bolted across the store and skidded on his knees beside her. The hell with the getaway car. Becca was his first priority.

By God, his hands shook as he touched her thigh, felt for injuries, took in the blood staining her temple.

She didn't even stir.

And that scared him. Badly.

"Becca Sue?" He brushed his knuckles over her cheek. "Come on, baby. Wake up." He felt inadequate and totally out of his element, a feeling he didn't experience often, and one he didn't like a bit. He started to reach for his cell phone, but paused when he saw movement behind her eyelids.

Her green eyes opened slowly, then snapped wide as confusion warred with recognition.

"What...? Colby?" She made a reflexive move to sit up, but he stopped her.

"Hey there, sugar pie." He tried to keep his tone light even though everything in him wanted to shout. "Lie still and let me check you out."

"I think somebody else tried to beat you to it." Her voice shook, and she flinched when he brushed her right side. "Nearly checked me out for good."

He caught her hand as she lifted it toward her head.

"Did you see his car?" she asked. "Get a plate number?"

"I'm a lawyer, not a cop." He gritted his teeth. "Damn it, Becca, you're bleeding."

"Excellent deduction, Sherlock. Do you have to make it sound like an accusation?"

"Sorry." He glanced around for something to staunch the flow, but he might as well have been blind, because his brain didn't register a single sight in the room but the ooze of crimson along Becca's temple. The hell with it.

Whipping off his T-shirt, he pressed it to her head. She groaned and he nearly jumped back. "Too hard?"

"No. You don't have to ruin your shirt. There are towels over by the coffee bar."

She was staring at his bare chest, and under any other circumstances he would have made something of it—at least teased her with a sexy remark. But he still hadn't gotten his spit back and his heart was pounding hard against his ribs.

"It's an old shirt. Do you hurt anywhere else?"

"My side. And my arm feels like it's on fire. I heard a noise and I thought Trouble was down here knocking over my merchandise. When I opened the door, someone hit me in the side. I think my arm and my hand took the brunt of it."

"It might be broken." Carefully, he ran his hand from her shoulder to her wrist, then over the delicate structure of her hand.

She yelped and he jerked back, the sound affecting him like a blow to the solar plexus. Whoever the bastard was, he'd taken more than one swing.

Not only was her head bleeding, but her wrist and hand were red and beginning to swell. "We need to get you to the hospital."

"Don't be going overboard, Colby. I've got ice and bandages upstairs." She started to sit up. Her face went ashen and she grabbed his forearm for support.

He quickly slid his arm beneath her shoulders, gently pushed her back down and resumed pressing his shirt against her head. "Just be still, would you?"

Palming his cell phone, he flipped through the stored numbers until he reached the one for the sheriff's office. He had enough presence of mind to know that dialing 9-1-1 would connect him to a dispatcher in Austin, who would then have to reroute his call to Hope Valley, and he wasn't in the mood to waste time.

He punched the button and waited for the sheriff's office to pick up, still keeping one hand pressed to Becca's forehead. His gut was in fist-size knots, and he was livid that someone had hurt Becca.

The strength of his protective feelings as he gazed down at her stunned him.

"Hope Valley sheriff's department."

"Margo, this is Colby Flynn. I'm over at Becca's Attic. There's been a break-in—"

"Is anyone hurt?" the dispatcher interrupted. "Becca Sue…? Is she all right?" Margo Reed ran the sheriff's department like a drill sergeant, yet governed herself by a set of rules she made up to suit any given situation. She also knew and loved just about everyone in town.

"Becca's a little banged up, but I'll be taking her to the clinic."

"Okay, hon. I'll get Skeeter right over there. And I'll call Storm at home. He's off duty tonight, but he'd skin me alive if I didn't let him know what was going on."

Colby knew the sheriff wasn't working—he'd passed by Anna's Café earlier this evening and seen Storm Carmichael and his family having a meal. Becca had been there, too.

Maybe it was because he was in the middle of packing to move, but Colby had suddenly felt like an outsider, and instead of stopping in to join the group of friends as he might have done at any other time, he'd kept on going.

"Thanks, Margo. Tell Storm not to come down this late. The perp's long gone. I'll file a report with the deputy, get Becca over to the clinic and call Storm tomorrow."

He folded the cell phone and dropped it back in his pocket, then lifted the corner of the makeshift pressure bandage and inspected Becca's cut.

"The bleeding has slowed. Do you know what you were hit with?"

"I only remember the blow to the side. I think I

might have hit my head on the corner of the book rack when I fell. Self-inflicted injury," she said, sounding embarrassed. "A bandage and some ice and I'll be as good as new."

"I don't think so, sugar pie. Getting knocked down is not self-inflicted. And I'm a pretty decent judge of broken bones, since I had my share as a kid. This wrist needs X-rays and a cast."

"Doggone it, Colby, I don't have time for a cast. I have a business to run and it takes *two* hands."

"Hey, don't shoot the messenger, darlin'." She'd always been stubborn and argumentative. If he hadn't been so upset, he might have even admired her pluck in this instance. But he *was* upset. More than he wanted to admit.

And having her right under his hands wearing thin cotton pajamas wasn't doing much to improve his mood. The pale yellow fabric was soft to the touch. The sleeveless top dipped in a fairly modest V-cut, and the pants hem hit about shin length. Nothing terribly erotic about the ensemble, yet judging by the way his body was responding, she might as well have been wearing a sheer negligee.

He reached for a magazine off the shelf, then grabbed a spool of orange ribbon. He had several yards reeled off and cut with his pocketknife almost before she could get her mouth open to object.

"What in the world are you doing? That ribbon's pure silk. And it's expensive."

"Put it on my bill," he snapped.

"As if," she said, rolling her eyes. "Ouch!"

"Sorry." He cupped the magazine around her arm, forming a makeshift splint, and secured one end of it with some ribbon. "I'm trying to be gentle. You could cooperate, you know."

With her free hand, she gripped the ends of the *Country Homes* magazine, bringing the page edges close together so he could get the rest of the ribbon wrapped around it and tied. "This just seems like overkill. Some ice and aspirin are all I need."

"No, you need to see a doctor, and I'd just as soon have your arm stabilized before we make the trip so you don't sustain any further injury."

"Since when did you become a medical expert?"

"Since I represented a woman in a domestic violence case. Husband was a repeat offender. I'd finally convinced her to leave him, but then she let him back in the door. She called me, and I got to the house in time to stop the worst of the attack. She insisted she was fine, but she stumbled against the wall, and the bone that was merely cracked before became badly fractured. The ER doc said if we'd immobilized the arm, the damage wouldn't have been as severe. Now, do you want to take the chance of standing up, getting woozy and falling, doing yourself more damage?"

"It annoys me when you take that condescending 'I'm right' tone."

"I know, darlin'. It always did."

Reminders of the past. He knew he shouldn't be going down that road, and thankfully, he was saved the trip when the deputy's cruiser pulled up out front.

"HELP ME SIT UP," Becca said, gripping Colby's wrist with her good hand. "I don't want Skeeter calling an ambulance or something." She was grateful for Colby's strong arm across her back. She just hoped he didn't make any more little innuendos about their past.

"You get any paler, and I'm going to call Mason and Damian myself."

She gave him an exasperated look. Typical of small towns, they knew their paramedics by name. Of course Becca had gone to school with the two men and Tracy Lynn had dated both of them before she'd married Lincoln Slade. In light of the friendship, she didn't particularly want Damian Stoltz or Mason Lowe checking her over while she was wearing her pajamas. That would be too weird.

"You'd just be wasting the county's resources," she said, noting that Skeeter was approaching the front glass door.

"Stay put," Colby said and rose. He crossed the shop to meet the deputy.

Becca wasn't about to stay put. For some reason, being injured and being the center of attention embarrassed her. She'd always taken care of herself, never had to rely on others. Now here she was with her head, her arm and her side throbbing, the pain making her nauseous. But she'd be darned if she'd lie on the floor as if she were a victim, never mind that she actually *was* one.

Slowly, she got to her knees and, using the wall to steady herself, she stood.

Colby was at her side in an instant. "I see you're

as hardheaded as ever." He assisted her over to one of the bistro chairs by the coffee service bar, and made her sit.

"Not too hardheaded," Skeeter said, indicating Colby's bloody T-shirt in her hand and the oozing wound at her head. "Want me to get the medics?"

Becca dabbed at the cut and applied pressure. It seemed to hurt less if she pressed hard. "No. I'm fine."

"I'm fixing to take her over to the emergency clinic," Colby said.

"Good idea." Skeeter nodded. "Either of you get a look at who did this?" He turned to Colby for an answer, but Becca was too tired to make an issue of it. Never mind that it was her shop and she was the one who'd been clobbered.

Colby shook his head. "When I got here, the alley door was forced open and Becca was in here on the floor. Unconscious."

He glanced at her, and Becca wondered why his tone held that hint of accusation. Sheesh, you'd think she'd done this on purpose just to irritate him!

"How'd you happen to just show up?" Skeeter asked.

"I was working late across the street, saw what looked like the beam of a flashlight and got suspicious. I didn't run into anyone on the way over here, and since you just came in through the front entrance, I assume whoever was in here heard me come around back and went out the front door. Once

I got inside, I heard a car engine—sounded like it was coming from around the corner."

Skeeter was writing on a pad of paper as Colby talked. "Was there anything about the vehicle's sound you can tell us? Did it sound like a diesel? An older car? Souped up?"

"Hard to tell. But I'd say the car may need a new muffler soon. I could clearly hear the engine turn over and the acceleration."

Becca was impressed with Colby's attention to detail. Good thing he'd been close by. She glanced around the shop, trying to see if anything obvious was missing. A round display rack had been tipped over, spilling paperback books across the floor. The beaded and faux gem bracelets that normally hung from the jewelry tree on the counter were in a tangled heap on the carpet.

It creeped her out that she'd been unconscious and some crazed idiot burglar had been pawing through her prized possessions.

And how long had Colby been hovering over her? she wondered. Had she done anything strange in her unconscious state?

She sighed. The knock on the head was making her think like a crazy person. It was just that she hated being vulnerable.

"Listen," Colby said, "do you mind if we do this report later? I need to get Becca to the clinic."

Becca wasn't going to argue now. Her hand was beginning to ache deep in the bone. And despite her sleeveless cotton pajamas, she was sweating.

But making it out the door anytime soon didn't seem to be in the cards.

A red Chevy Tahoe pulled up at the front curb. Donetta Carmichael hopped out of the SUV almost before it had come to a stop and came barreling through the front door of Becca's Attic. Her long, wildly curling red hair was scraped into a fashionably messy ponytail that somehow looked as though she'd spent hours making it look that way. Then again, Donetta owned the only hair salon in town, just two doors down from Becca's Attic, so she *should* know how to fix her hair all cute at a moment's notice.

"Lord, Becca Sue! Are you all right? My God! What happened?" Donetta knelt in front of Becca, touching her face and patting her thighs, as though she didn't quite know what to do or how to do it. "Skeeter? Have you called the paramedics?" She didn't wait for Skeeter's reply. Instead, she blasted her husband as he came through the door carrying an infant swaddled in a fluffy pink blanket. "Storm, call Mason and Damian. Becca Sue's hurt."

"Netta," Becca soothed, putting her hand on Donetta's shoulder, "I'm okay. It's just a little bump on the head. The way everyone's acting, you'd think I looked like a bloody corpse." Maybe she should go have a look at herself in the bathroom mirror, Becca thought.

"Oh, don't even talk about corpses at a time like this!"

Becca rolled her eyes and was instantly sorry. An

invisible demon was having a heyday jabbing a pitchfork at her temple. "You didn't have to drag your family out in the middle of the night, Donetta."

"As if I'd stay home snug in my bed when my best friend is bleeding all over the floor. Who would come in here and attack you like this?"

"Lord, you're as big a drama queen as Colby."

"Colby?" For the first time since she'd charged through the front door, Donetta looked around the room. Her gaze landed on Colby—who was shirtless—then shifted back to Becca. Now, instead of stark worry, there was an impish spark of feminine appreciation that seemed to say, *Well, well. Lookie here.*

"Don't start," Becca whispered. "He was working late and saw a flashlight beam in my store. I think he scared the intruder away."

"Um, sweetheart?" Storm said. The sheriff now stood just behind his wife, holding the deputy's notes in one hand, the baby in the crook of his other arm. "I'm the one who should be asking questions. If you'll take the baby, perhaps I can at least *try* to act like the sheriff?"

"Actually," Colby interrupted, "I'd appreciate it if we could handle any reports and statements tomorrow. I'd really like to get Becca to the clinic."

"Yes," Donetta said, standing, "that's exactly what you should do. Storm can wait." She blithely took over, dismissing her husband's attempts to do his job. Storm merely gazed down at his wife with loving indulgence.

"Do you want me to follow you to the clinic?" Donetta asked. "I've called Tracy Lynn and Sunny—"

"Call them back!" Becca demanded. Realizing she'd practically shouted, she spoke in a more normal, rational tone. "Please, Netta. There's no reason for everyone to be burning up the highway for nothing. You go home and get the baby back to bed."

She couldn't resist standing on tiptoe and taking a peek at the sweet little girl sleeping in her daddy's arm. Amanda Skye Carmichael was four months old, and if the scant hair on her soft head was any indication, it looked as though she would be a redhead like her mommy.

"Besides," she continued, "Colby's already awake and apparently fairly traumatized, so he may as well drive me over to see the doc. Maybe they'll give him a shot of something to calm *him* down." She glanced at Colby and her stomach flipped when she saw the amused tug of his lips—not to mention his bare chest.

She grabbed a clean dish towel from the drawer behind the coffee counter, then apologetically passed him his bloodstained T-shirt.

The thought of spending more time with Colby was seriously taxing her nerves. If it weren't for the baby, she would have *definitely* taken Donetta up on her offer to go to the hospital with her.

Colby put his arm around her. "Before I get even *more* traumatized," he drawled, his eyebrows lifting, "shall we go?"

"Let me just change my clothes."

"Forget it, darlin'. You're not stalling another minute."

"I'm wearing pajamas!" And *he* still hadn't put on his darn shirt. Although she couldn't really expect him to wear it now with her blood all over it.

"I'll run upstairs and get your robe," Donetta said.

Before Becca could object, Donetta was heading for the stairwell.

"Call Tracy Lynn and Sunny," Becca shouted after her. "And grab my purse while you're up there. Sheesh," she said, glancing at Colby. "All this fuss I hate having people do stuff I can easily do myself."

"*Easily* is the operative word, sugar." He glanced pointedly at the hand she was cradling close to her chest. "Let us fuss a little. Makes us feel better."

His Southern drawl certainly made *her* feel… something. She just wasn't sure if it was better.

Chapter Three

"I don't know why this sling thing is necessary." Leaving the clinic, Becca adjusted the material that was chafing her neck and stepped aside as Colby opened the door of his SUV. "I feel ridiculous."

"Quit being a baby, sugar pie, and get in the truck." Without waiting for her to comply, he tossed her purse into the cab, then put his hands at her waist and hoisted her into the seat. "You're damned lucky your injuries weren't worse."

He shut the passenger door, preventing her from leveling a comeback. So, okay, she was being difficult. But darn it, she didn't have time for this nonsense! She *never* got sick or hurt.

And the last thing she needed was this slow-talking, Matthew McConaughey look-alike hovering over her, making her long for the elusive, grand passion that had once burned red-hot, yet had sputtered out, smothered by a blanket of youth and opposing goals.

She hadn't realized until just now that she was holding a grudge.

Still, she *had* gotten a kick out of him carrying her purse through the clinic. He hadn't batted an eye, showing he was completely comfortable with his masculinity. Thankfully, he'd had a clean shirt in his truck that he'd pulled on, saving her and the clinic staff from drooling.

At 2:00 a.m. the Hope Valley Emergency Medical Clinic had been practically deserted, so it had only taken about forty-five minutes to get X-rays and treatment. The bone on the side of her right hand just below her wrist appeared to have a hairline fracture. For something that was hardly visible on the X-ray film, Becca thought, it sure hurt like the devil.

In place of the magazine Colby had cribbed from the store, she now wore a splint that covered her from knuckles to elbow. The foam-and-fiberglass contraption was held in place by a wad of Ace bandages that made it look as though she had a hugely serious injury. The doctor hadn't felt she needed a cast at this point, but would reassess in a few days after the swelling had subsided.

Meanwhile, her hand ached and she felt like a cranky bird with a broken wing. Heck, the eight stitches in her forehead were hardly worth a mention. Granted the gash stung, but at least that injury didn't get in the way of anything.

"This sling's gotta go," she remarked when Colby slid into the driver's seat and started the truck.

He shot her a look of exasperation and didn't bother to argue. Instead, he leaned over, pulled the seat belt across her chest and buckled it at her hip, taking extra care to make sure the belt didn't press against her injured arm.

Becca shivered and wondered if he'd deliberately let his fingers linger against her skin, or if she'd just imagined the caress. Colby *had* been acting strangely lately.

She turned her head and reached across her body, using her left hand to lower the window a couple of inches.

Main Street was quiet and dark as they traveled the short distance from the clinic back to Becca's. A warm summer breeze wafted in through the crack in the window, perfumed by the scent of alfalfa fields in the distance and fresh earth, still damp from an earlier rainstorm that had dumped just enough moisture to turn the streets steamy and bring out the mosquitoes.

The threadbare chenille robe draped over her shoulders wasn't needed for warmth, and it hadn't done much good for modesty, either. Thank heaven her pajamas were decent.

"I still can't believe someone broke in to my shop."

"You've got merchandise that's easy to turn. I'm surprised you haven't been hit before."

"Well, Donetta popped me in the stomach once, but it was an accident. She'd been aiming at a basketball hoop and I got in the way."

His eyebrows slammed together and his jaw tightened. "I didn't mean 'hit' in that context, and you know it."

Becca rolled her eyes. Clearly he couldn't take a joke. "You don't need to snap."

He took a deep, audible breath and let it out. "What is it with you and me?"

"Oil and water?" she asked, knowing right away that he was talking about their past and their inability to get through more than a day peacefully.

He parked in the alleyway behind her store and shut off the engine. In the moment of quiet, where the only sound was the ticking noise of the hot engine cooling down, he said softly, "We mix better than oil and water, sugar pie."

"Then why are we apart?" The words were out before she could call them back. A warm flush of embarrassment washed over her and she wanted to slide right off the seat. But to take back the words would only call more attention to them, lend them more strength. Still... "Never mind. That was a dumb thing to say."

"We're not really apart," he said. "Friendship should count for something."

"It does." Thank goodness he didn't take a trip down the ex-lovers' path. "And I appreciate your being here for me tonight. I know I'm grouchy, but I'm not ungrateful."

He reached over and stroked a finger down her cheek. "I remember that about you, sugar. You have one of the sweetest hearts of anyone I've ever met."

Oh, when he said things like that, touched her like that... *Becca Sue. Get a grip. He's only being nice.*

"Um...thank you. I suppose I should go in and check things out."

"Stay put." He got out of the truck and came

around to her side, opening the door and helping her alight. "We don't need to check anything out tonight. The morning's soon enough."

"Colby, there's no way I can sleep knowing someone's been pawing through my shop." The alleyway behind her store was pitch-black. Obviously, whoever had broken in had disabled the motion detector light over the back door. She had installed the light for convenience purposes, mainly so she could see to get her key in the lock. Until tonight, she'd never considered security measures a necessity. Not in a town like Hope Valley, the place she'd lived all her life.

Becca stood on tiptoe, trying to reach the bulb, hoping it was only unscrewed.

"Damn it, Becca Sue." Colby gently lowered her arm and took care of it himself. The light blinked on, flooding them in a pool of white. "You make it difficult for a man to show his chivalry."

She nearly snorted. "Guess I'm just set in my single, independent ways. No big strong man to open my pickle jars, troubleshoot my circuit breakers or screw in my lightbulbs."

"Then I imagine we're going to butt heads for the next little while. Did you bring the keys to your front door? Looks like Skeeter boarded up this one after he left."

She started to ask about his butting-heads comment, but got sidetracked by the wood nailed across her shop's back door. She frowned. "A lot of good it does with the boards on the outside. Anyone could just pry them off."

"Which is what Skeeter was probably thinking when he put them here rather than on the inside. They'll slow down an intruder, but if you'd forgotten your front door keys in all the excitement, you wouldn't be locked out."

"Oh. Good thinking."

"*Do* you have your keys?"

"Yes." She nodded to the satchel-like purse he had stuffed under his arm, the handles riding his shoulder. "They're in there."

He unzipped the leather and she reached in with her good hand, digging around the bottom until she felt metal. She pulled out an antique broach attached to a huge safety pin with keys dangling from it, then dropped them back in the purse and continued to feel around.

"Those weren't them?" Colby asked.

"No. Just spares I keep for Donetta and Tracy Lynn and Sunny. We all have keys to each other's places." She felt metal and grasped it. Same set of keys. Before she could let go, Colby snatched them from her.

"I'll just hold these, why don't I? The sun'll be up soon and folks might talk if we're caught standing outside with you in your pajamas, cute as they may be."

She gave him a dirty look. "If I could hold the purse myself, I could put my hand right on the keys. At this awkward angle, I can't tell what I'm doing."

"Maybe you should think about cleaning out your purse or getting a smaller one. This thing's so heavy, it's a wonder you can carry it without walking crooked."

She found the keys and held them up as if they were a prize. "If it's too heavy for you, I'll be happy to take it," she said sweetly.

"Smart aleck. I think I can manage." He slid the bag back onto his shoulder, put his arm around her and steered her around the corner toward the front sidewalk. "You'd be doing yourself a favor, though, by getting something that's only *half* the size of a suitcase."

"Actually, I've tried a bunch of times to downsize. Made me feel naked and vulnerable. I end up cramming everything into the little purse until it's bulging and won't close, then the big one sits there taunting me, still half-full with stuff that I'm afraid I might need once I leave the house."

Colby stared down at her as if he couldn't decide whether to laugh or beat his head against a wall. "Looked to me like there's a whole lot of junk in there—in quantity. Where are you going to go that you'll use *seven* pens?"

"Sunny's baby shower," she retorted without a blink. They rounded the corner to the front sidewalk. "We ran short of pencils for the baby-name game and I happened to be prepared with enough extra to go around."

Becca saw him open his mouth to comment, but just then Skeeter cruised by in the sheriff's sedan and rolled to a stop, leaning over to speak through the open window.

"How'd it go at the clinic, Becca Sue?"

She flapped her sling, wincing a bit when pain shot up her arm. "A hairline fracture in my hand. Nothing to worry about."

"How about your head?" Skeeter asked. "Looked to me like the bastard clocked you a good one."

"I'm pretty sure I did that myself when I fell."

"With a little help," Colby and Skeeter said at the same time.

Becca sighed, glancing at the tight-lipped expressions on both men's faces. Under different circumstances, she might enjoy two guys fussing over her.

The news had spread like wildfire among her best friends, and her cell phone had rung nonstop on the way to the clinic—and even inside the clinic, much to the night nurse's annoyance. Even though Donetta had been at the shop and they'd talked face-to-face, she'd phoned for an update before Becca had even seen the doctor. Tracy Lynn had called twice and so had Sunny. It had been all Becca could do to assure her friends that she was fine and that they should *not* drag their babies and families and pregnant selves out in the middle of the night to hold her hand.

Funny how their objections had lessened considerably when she'd told them Colby was with her.

"I'll let you two get inside to rest," Skeeter said. "Storm'll be by tomorrow to do an official report on anything that's missing. Expect a call from Beth, too," he added, his gaze on Becca. "I'll let her know you're fine, but you know how she is. Frets over everyone."

"Thanks, Skeeter. You tell Beth not to worry about me. She's got enough on her hands with Landon's summer cold." Skeeter and his wife had a ten-month-old little boy with big blue eyes and curly brown hair—the spitting image of his daddy. Becca had seen them in the pharmacy just yesterday and she hadn't been able to resist cupping his flushed cheeks....

She wished she had a slice of the family pie so many of her friends were enjoying. They had husbands who came home to them at the end of the day, children to nurture and hold close, help changing lightbulbs and unstopping toilets and picking up the slack when life suddenly became overwhelming.

"You okay, sugar pie?"

Becca shook herself out of her musings, and realized that Skeeter was driving away. "Just peachy."

"Sounds like someone could use some pain meds," Colby said.

"Someone? Well, you go on ahead. I think I'll just tough it out."

"I'm not the enemy here, sugar."

"Damn it all, Colby, I know that. And I'm sorry." And doggone it, if she didn't watch herself, she was going to start bawling like a baby. Her hand *and* her head were hurting.

And her heart was feeling a few twinges, too. Compliments of the way-too-sexy Southern gentleman at her side who looked as though he were fixing to sweep her up and carry her, lest she fall out in a faint or something.

Bickering and holding Colby at arm's length was one thing. Allowing him close when he had that gentle, I'm-your-man look in his eyes was quite another.

He made her yearn for what she didn't have. Couldn't have…with him.

"Let me have your keys, sugar pie, and we'll get you inside."

She didn't have the energy to argue, so she passed him the keys and went through the door when he swung it open, using her good hand to flip on the light switch. She noticed that Skeeter had lowered the shades over the front windows.

"Oh, my gosh. Look at all this black dust. It'll take me forever to get it off everything!"

"Yeah, fingerprinting dust is messy."

"You'd think Skeeter would've at least cleaned up behind himself."

"Not his job, sugar pie."

"Oh, just hush up. You've always got to be so darned reasonable." She marched to the coffee counter, grabbed the end of the paper towel roll and gave it a jerk, not wholly sure why she was so snippy with him.

Colby easily took the towel away from her. "We're not going to start on this tonight. You need to elevate your arm and get some rest."

"I can't rest knowing this mess is down here."

"It's not going anywhere."

"Exactly. And I open at nine in the morning."

"I think the town would understand if you closed up shop for a couple of days."

"The town might, but my bank account certainly wouldn't."

"Don't you have a cushion for emergencies?"

She looked away. "I've got some savings, but I don't consider this enough of an emergency to dip into it. Besides, I need to see if anything's missing."

"We'll deal with it tomorrow." He steered her toward the interior stairs that led to her upstairs apartment.

"What do you mean, 'we'?" She glanced back, her gaze touching on a Chippendale tall-case clock in the corner, a display of Victorian glassware along the wall, a pair of French nineteenth-century Napoleon III gilt and bronze torches, old wooden shelves and round racks stuffed with books. Skeeter had at least picked up the display rack that had fallen, but there was no telling what order the books were in.

"Judging by all the things you've been whining about in the past few hours, you're going to need some help."

Her attention snapped back to Colby. "I haven't been whining. I've been bitching. There's a difference."

"Mmm. That's what I meant, but I was trying to be polite in light of your infirmary."

"Oh, stop with the infirmary and invalid stuff. And why you?"

"Why me, what?"

"Why would you help me?"

"Why not?"

"I can see we're getting really far with this conversation," she drawled in exasperation. Taking one last glance around the shop, she stopped and whirled, gasping when her arm connected with Colby's chest.

"Trouble! Oh, baby cakes. Come down to Mom." Despite the jolt of pure pain that shot up her arm, she pushed past Colby and headed to the front counter. Her cat was perched atop the Victorian, cabbage-rose valance that spanned the length of the front windows. Trouble, a small, sleek black cat, was so named because his curiosity more often than not got him in trouble.

After a few swishes of his tail, he finally leaped atop a bookshelf, navigated an antique hall tree, then dropped to the countertop and sashayed over to her, picking his way through the costume jewelry that had been retrieved from the floor and piled on the counter.

"Have you been in here all along?" she crooned, scooping the cat up with her good arm. "Poor baby. You were probably scared half to pieces. Too bad you can't tell Mom who was in our shop." She plunked a kiss on his ebony head. "And I apologize for accusing you falsely."

Colby stood by the stairwell door, his arms crossed over his chest. Watching her.

"What? You don't talk to your animals?" she asked and made her way back to him.

"Don't have any."

She frowned. "What about Bosco?" The boxer/Lab mix was practically a fixture at his side most days.

"Bosco died last week."

"No!" Her steps faltered. "Sunny would have told me."

"I haven't said anything to her. I took him with me to Houston last week and snuck him into the motel room. Bosco went to sleep and didn't wake up the next morning."

"Oh, Colby, I'm so sorry."

"Yeah. Me, too. It was his time, though. He was half-blind and suffering some from arthritis. When it's my time, I'd just as soon go like Bosco—peacefully in my sleep. Here, let me have this little menace." He reached out and took Trouble from her, then guided her up the stairs—successfully this time.

As they entered the apartment, the scent of the cinnamon buns she'd prepared earlier that evening lingered in the air, making the small space feel homey and welcoming.

Thank goodness she'd baked an extra batch to put in the freezer and had another batch ready to pop in the oven first thing in the morning. But what would she do after that? It took two good hands to knead bread dough.

Normally she could count on her girlfriends to help out, but Sunny was fixing to have a baby any day now, and Tracy Lynn and Donetta had infants to care for.

Things had changed so much in the past year or so. Sunny Carmichael had come back home and married her high school sweetheart, Jack Slade, and had legally adopted his seven-year-old daughter, Tori. Now they were about to have a baby together. Becca was on pins and needles waiting for the call since Sunny was actually past her due date, and Jack was like a nervous lion hovering over its cub because Sunny, as the town's only veterinarian, still insisted on working.

Then Donetta had fallen in love with Sunny's brother, Storm Carmichael, and they'd had a baby girl four months ago. Donetta's beauty salon had now, more than ever, become the hangout for all and sundry who had a soft spot for babies. Donetta had turned the back room into a makeshift nursery, complete with bassinets, a changing table and a couple of rocking chairs. There was never a shortage of willing babysitters.

Tracy Lynn had ended up marrying Jack Slade's brother, Linc. Now *there* was a union that hadn't seemed likely. The socialite and the bad-boy horse breeder. They were the perfect fit for each other, though, and now they were the proud parents of a two-month-old baby girl.

Their lives had definitely taken drastic—yet wonderful—turns. Once again, Becca felt that small pinch of envy as she thought about her three friends experiencing pregnancy together. And she could only watch, listen and yearn....

And find herself stuck with Colby Flynn in the close confines of her apartment—without the buffer of her girlfriends.

"Ready for bed?" Colby asked.

Becca whipped around and nearly lost her balance. "Are you doing that deliberately?"

"What?"

"Making sexual innuendos."

"Darlin', I don't know where your mind is, but I was merely attempting to follow the doc's orders. He said for the next twenty-four to seventy-two hours, rest and elevation are what'll speed the healing process for this hand."

"Seventy-two hours! He did not say that."

"'Fraid so. Those were his exact words to me while the nurse was helping you in the bathroom. Seeing as it's two-thirty in the morning, I'm thinking your bed is the best place to obey the doctor's orders." He tipped her chin up with a single finger, then lowered his voice. "And darlin'? When I make a sexual remark you'll know it. And it won't be couched in innuendo."

His lips brushed against hers, so softly, so quickly, that it left her stunned. She looked into his eyes. Yes, there was a spark of devilry there. But there was also something deeper. Something she couldn't quite define—and wasn't sure she even wanted to try.

What was he up to?

Colby Flynn had broken her heart once already. And once in a lifetime was enough.

She stepped back and cleared her throat. "Um, thanks for bringing me home. I can handle things from here."

"Did I not make myself clear? As soon as I get you settled, I intend to camp out on your couch."

"That's not—"

"Becca Sue, the lock on the back door to your shop is busted and the inside door leading up to this apartment is so flimsy a kid could kick it open. Damn it, seeing you bleeding on the floor took ten years off my life, so why don't you save your arguments and your breath, and let me do my Southern gentleman thing and hang around to make sure you're protected from any more bumps in the night."

His voice had risen, but she decided not to point that out. Besides, she'd forgotten about the flimsily boarded-up back door. Normally, she wouldn't care one way or the other if her doors were locked— Hope Valley simply didn't have a lot of crime.

But there had been a crime committed this evening—if not a robbery, at least an assault. And truth be told, she was shaken.

Shaken and hurting. And clumsy, all trussed up like a Thanksgiving turkey. Well, one arm, anyway.

She took a breath and nodded. He wasn't a man who would easily budge once he had his mind set on something.

He closed and locked the interior door, lowered Trouble to the floor and steered Becca into the bedroom.

Sliding the robe from her shoulders, he held back the covers as she got into bed, then piled every pillow she owned around her and under her arm.

There were a couple of small bloodstains on her pajamas, but she was too exhausted to tackle the chore of changing clothes.

"Are you hungry?" he asked.

She shook her head, not quite sure how she felt about all this attention.

And Colby Flynn in her bedroom.

"You're supposed to take this pain medication with food. When did you eat last?"

"Supper."

"That was a long time ago. I'll go fix you some soup and get an ice pack for your hand."

"Okay," she said. "I know darn well you're not the nursemaid type. So what's with you all of a sudden?"

He cocked an eyebrow, a sexy challenge, and drawled, "I wouldn't say it's all of a sudden, darlin'. We do go back a ways."

She waved her uninjured hand dismissively. "Bless it all, Colby. You know what I mean. We lived together, for goodness sake. You moved away, but you've been back more than a little while. Criminy, you've had your office across the street from me for almost a year. In all this time, you've not felt the need to coddle me or butt into my life."

"You think I'm butting in?"

"Aren't you?"

"Some would call it friendship."

"I have plenty of friends. I certainly don't need…" She stopped before she went too far.

"What don't you need?" he asked softly, making

it clear that she *had* gone too far. He stepped closer, ran his thumb over the curve of her jaw, gently skimmed the bandage over her forehead. "Or maybe I should ask what it is that you *do* need?"

Darn it, she wished he'd keep his hands to himself. What she needed was a husband, a lover, a father for the children she wanted to have.

"I need two good working hands and a batch of bread dough."

"Bread dough?"

"You don't think the rolls and pastries I sell come from the supermarket, do you?"

"I guess I never really thought about it. You make all that stuff by hand?"

"With *two* hands, yes."

"Looks like you have a problem, then."

"That's what I've been trying to tell you."

He shrugged. "Guess it won't hurt the town to go on a diet for a few weeks."

"I do a brisk business in pastries. Some days, I sell as much at the coffee-and-pastry bar as I do on the antiques-and-books side of the shop. I can't afford to force a diet on the citizens of Hope Valley."

"Okay, how hard can it be? I can help you stir up some stuff."

The idea both stunned and tickled her. "You're kidding, right?"

"Don't look so shocked. I happen to own an apron or two."

Lord love a duck. If Colby Flynn was going to don an apron in her kitchen, she wanted pictures.

Chapter Four

"As much as I'd like to see you up to your eyeballs in flour," Becca said, "I'm pretty well done in for the night…or is it morning?"

He checked his gold watch. "It's 3:00 a.m."

She nearly groaned. "I might have to open late in the morning. It'll take a while to check the merchandise, see if anything's missing. I've already baked cinnamon rolls, and I've got some zucchini bread in the freezer that I can thaw. That should get me through the afternoon."

"I don't think anyone's going to starve, sugar. Anna's Café is just down the street, and if a person's desperate, they can grab a candy bar from Chandler's drugstore."

She smiled at him and settled into the pillows. "Won't be as good as my scones."

"Nothing's as good as your scones. The food that comes out of your oven is pure heaven."

She was touched by the compliment. "Thank you."

"How's your arm?" he asked, tucking the pillow more tightly under her elbow, making sure it was higher than the rest of her body.

"My wrist and my hand are aching pretty bad."

"Sit tight. I'll go get the soup and ice pack."

"Don't bother with the soup. I'm really not hungry."

He left the room without commenting. Becca was tired, but her hand was truly throbbing. She looked around the room to see where Colby had put the sack she'd gotten from the clinic. Since the pharmacy wasn't open until morning, the doctor had given her samples of pain medication—enough to get her through a couple of days.

Naturally, the sack was nowhere in sight. And she didn't have the energy to get up and go in search of it. Besides, Colby had practically built a fort around her with the pillows. She was totally snug and didn't want to move because the pillows were supporting her just right, lessening the pressure on her bruised side.

Lord, this felt awkward. Here it was, the middle of the night—or wee hours of the morning—and she was alone in her apartment with Colby Flynn. Mere hours ago, she'd been watching him outside her window, ducking behind the curtains, wondering if he was watching her, too, wondering if he was thinking about making babies with her.

Criminy, Becca Sue. Get a grip!

There was no time to start fantasizing about Colby Flynn eyeing her with ulterior motives.

Silly ulterior motives based on a baby pact made when they'd both been drunk as skunks.

Her heart somersaulted when Colby walked back into the room carrying an ice pack and a sleeve of saltines. He sat on the side of the bed and gently laid the ice pack over her wrist, then held a cracker to her lips.

She shook her head.

"Open. You gotta eat something before you take this pain medication. Since you nixed the soup, this is your other option."

She took the cracker from him, shoved it in her mouth, chewed and swallowed. "There. Now hand over the drugs."

He grinned and produced the pills, along with a bottle of water. "Yes, ma'am."

She took the pills and settled back against the pillows. Colby didn't seem in a hurry to leave, and if Becca were honest with herself, she would admit she wanted him to stay.

"It seems so surreal that someone actually hit me. I would have never imagined something like that happening in Hope Valley. We don't have crime here."

"Actually, we do, or I would have been out of a job long ago."

She noticed that his tone was edged with anger, his eyes hard as he glanced at her arm, then at her head. When they'd been together before—seven years ago—she hadn't seen this protective streak of his.

"What were you doing at the office so late tonight?" she asked.

"Packing."

"For what?"

"Moving to Dallas."

A deflating sensation, like a balloon that had suddenly been pricked by a pin, stole her breath. And she had no business feeling this way.

"I guess I didn't realize… I'd heard Darla Pam talking about you, but I just figured she was gossiping so I didn't pay attention." Actually, she hadn't wanted to pay attention. She'd felt so sure that Darla Pam was wrong. With news as important as this, Becca had been nearly positive that Colby would have given *her* a heads-up before he let it become the talk of the town.

Again, she wondered why she was thinking along these lines. Colby's life was none of her business. It hadn't been for many long years. They'd both moved on. She'd dated several guys in the interim— alas, no Mr. Right in the bunch—and even though she'd never actually seen Colby with a woman since he'd had his law office across the street from her, she was sure he, too, maintained an active social life. Especially during the years he'd been away from Hope Valley.

"I got an offer for a partnership at a law firm in Dallas. It was too good to pass up."

The idea of him moving away again should not have given her such a pang of disappointment. "Well, if that's what you want, then I'm happy for you."

Lamplight glanced off the crystal face of his gold watch—the very watch she'd given him just last week. She'd found the watch at a pawnshop and had noticed the engraved name on the casing— D. J. McGee. Since she'd always been into family history, she'd naturally looked into Colby's. The initials on the back of the watch led her to believe that it had once belonged to Colby's great-grandfather, Daniel James McGee.

Figuring he would want the heirloom, she'd packaged it up, along with a note, and mailed it to him.

There was no denying that her delivery method had squawked like a plucked chicken.

"How come you didn't bring the watch over yourself?" he asked, obviously noticing the direction of her stare.

"How come you thanked me by mail?" she countered, not wanting to admit that she'd hoped he would seek her out, if only to talk about the watch.

"Touché," he said quietly. "Ever wonder why we do so much of that? Tiptoeing around each other?"

She shrugged, feeling the strap of the sling dig into her shoulder.

"Suppose it's because we've seen each other naked?" he asked.

"Colby!" She felt heat rush to her cheeks.

He grinned. "Well, it's true."

"That was a long time ago."

"I've got a good memory."

She glanced away—not because she was embarrassed, but because thoughts of the past made her sad. No matter how much she wished things were different, they weren't.

She was still single and childless.

Colby was still reaching for his own brass ring.

The fact that they were both, very clearly, still attracted to one another didn't change anything.

He put a finger under her chin. "Hey. You okay?"

No. She was not. Her head hurt, her side and her hand hurt, and Colby intended to move to Dallas.

"When you left…before—" *when you dumped me,* she wanted to say, but didn't "—you said you wanted a fancy career, power and recognition. If you were so ambitious and money-conscious, why'd you come back to Hope Valley?"

"Having a private law practice is nothing to sneeze at, darlin'."

"It wasn't good enough for you back then."

"Dude Wayland was still here and in business. Until he retired, there wasn't room for two law firms."

Colby set the sleeve of crackers on Becca's nightstand. He knew he was evading her question, but he wasn't keen on examining his motives quite so deeply, nor sharing them with Becca.

She yawned and he jumped at the chance to sidestep this conversation. "Pain meds kicking in?" he asked.

"Probably."

"You'd better get some sleep." He stood and tucked the sheet around her. "Want the window left open?"

"No. If you don't mind shutting it and turning on the fan, that'd be great."

He saw the wariness in her eyes, knew she was thinking about the intruder. He lowered the casement window and pulled the shade that was tucked up under the sheer Priscilla curtains, then tugged the chain on the overhead fan. "Better?" he asked.

She nodded. "Thanks."

He started back toward the bed, then stopped because he didn't wholly trust himself. He wanted to kiss her and make her wounds better, hold her and ease her fears.

But he'd given up that right a long time ago. And since he hadn't changed his mind about his reasons, he had no business playing with their emotions, either hers or his. The problem was, he couldn't seem to help himself.

"You sleep, sugar. I'll be right out here on the couch."

"You don't need to stay, Colby."

"Hush now, and go to sleep, tough girl."

He backed out of the room and pulled the door halfway closed. It wasn't likely that he'd fit well on the sofa, but that was his only choice, other than the floor or Becca's bed. The latter wasn't an option.

As he rummaged through the linen closet for a blanket and pillow, he thought about her question.

When he'd come back to Hope Valley, it *had* represented prestige to him. He'd still been in Houston when Donetta had called and asked him to handle her divorce—she didn't want folks in town knowing her business, that her sleazy husband at the time, the model-perfect public citizen, the town's respected banker, was abusing her. That was around the time Colby had gotten the sappy idea about coming back to his hometown and being the hero—righting wrongs and untangling legal messes.

Instead, he'd been tortured by the presence of Becca Sue, by what he'd had and thrown away.

Now here he was, teetering on the wave of change. His monetary ship had come in—or was waiting at the dock for him to board. The partnership with Wells and Steadman was a *very* prestigious career move, a guaranteed salary of three times what he could make here in private practice.

The offer had come about through the senior partner's daughter, a woman he'd dated off and on over the past couple of years. Nothing serious— although he suspected Cassandra might not object to it becoming so.

Cassandra Wells was the opposite of Becca Sue. Where Becca was soft-hearted and sweet, with a compact body and a love of family and history and home and hearth, Cassandra was a workaholic like him, tall and statuesque, her total focus on getting ahead. She was friendly, but could easily become a shark. Worldly, gorgeous and scrupulously organized. Hell, on the surface, she was perfect for him.

He shoved a pillow and blanket under his arm and glanced into Becca's room once more. She was sound asleep.

Unable to help himself, he stepped farther into the room. The light from the hall spilled over her pale face, illuminating the dark hair feathering her cheek. He noted the robe lying next to her bed, the jewelry and discarded coffee cup on top of the dresser, shoes under the chair, a tote bag next to it filled with yarn and knitting supplies. A half-burned candle that would probably drip wax if it were relit sat atop the cedar chest, and three different kinds of lotion were on the bedside table, along with an untidy stack of books and magazines, each with a bookmark, business card or scrap of paper marking the spot where she'd left off reading.

It was all he could do not to pick up after her, find a place out of sight for all her things.

On the other hand, with its handmade quilts, harlequin masks and feathers hanging on the wall, and the framed photos and collectibles lining the marble-top dresser, this room looked and felt lived in. It was warm, colorful, eclectic. He couldn't imagine her with white furniture or glass-and-chrome tables that displayed only sparse pieces of expensive art.

Like the rooms of Cassandra's elegant town house in Dallas.

No, Becca Sue was by no means elegant. If he suggested such a thing, she'd probably slap him for being stupid.

She was, however, unique. She surrounded herself with people and possessions that brought her pleasure. She considered her little groupings of treasures cherished friends. He still didn't understand

how she could sell stuff she'd formed such attach-
ments to.

One thing he knew for sure by looking around
her apartment was that she could definitely use a
helping hand.

That was what he was here for.

WHEN BECCA awoke the next morning, she was sure
that she'd been run over by a semi and that the guy
had backed up and had a second go of it just to make
sure he got the job done right. It took a few minutes
for her fuzzy brain to summon up the events that had
put her in this state.

Someone had actually broken in to her shop.

Malicious burglary was so unheard of in a town
like Hope Valley that she wondered for a moment if
she'd dreamed it. But the aches and pains all over her
body told her that last night's drama had been very
real.

She clutched at the sheet and glanced at the
closed window. Normally, it would have been open,
letting in the summer breeze and the morning's
birdsong. But the sense of safety and security she'd
always taken for granted had been shaken. But, darn
it, she wasn't going to let some lowlife get the best
of her.

A noise from her kitchen made her freeze. It
sounded like someone rummaging through her cupboards. Every muscle in her body went rigid.

Then she remembered.

Colby.

Colby Flynn had spent the night with her.

He'd touched her, run his hands over her body. So, okay, he'd been checking for broken bones and injuries. Still…

A part of her felt giddy with excitement knowing he was just in the other room. Another part of her was scared to death. Colby Flynn was very dangerous to her peace of mind—and her good sense.

Right now, her good sense told her she'd better get up and get moving. The shop was due to open at nine.

For the first time in as long as she could remember, she wasn't looking forward to going to work. Normally the store was her sanctuary, one of the things in life that gave her incredible joy.

But today she felt like roadkill. And she'd barely had four hours of sleep. If that weren't enough, she had no idea what kind of mess she'd face in the light of day, and didn't relish the tedious job of inventorying her merchandise to determine the extent of her loss. But at least she *had* insurance.

Rolling to her side, fighting her way through the mound of pillows, she got out of bed and decided to go sit in the bathtub, see if that would ease her soreness. It felt as though her entire body had been beaten up, not just her side, her hand and her head.

Despite some difficulty getting comfortable last night, she'd finally dozed off and ended up sleeping like the dead. Those were some powerful pain pills. She still felt woozy this morning.

Her apartment only had one bedroom, but it had

two baths—one of them attached to her bedroom—
so she didn't have to worry about darting through the
hall or running into Colby before she was good and
ready. Closing the bathroom door behind her, she
turned on the hot water in the tub, adjusted the temperature, then plugged the drain and poured in
scented bath salts. Draped over the edge of the tub
was a plastic bag. Colby's doing, she knew, so that
she wouldn't get her splint wet. Did the man think
of everything?

She eased the blue sling over her head, then
quickly sat on the commode when a wave of dizzi-
ness hit her. Without the sling, her arm felt vulnerable. Breathing deeply, she waited until the weird
sensation passed, then unbuttoned her pajama top
and slipped it off. She had to tug a bit because the
armhole kept getting caught on the bulk of the Ace
bandage wrapped around the plastic-and-metal
splint. Getting her pajama bottoms off one-handed
wasn't as easy, either, but she managed by using her
feet to step on the hems.

She wrapped her splint with the plastic bag and
lowered herself into the fragrant, steamy water, awkwardly holding her right arm up. Thankfully, the tub
was situated so that her arm could rest on the outside
of the rim rather than the inside wall. She used her
toe to turn off the lever-style tap, and tried to immerse
as much of her body in the hot water as she could,
hoping to soak the aches away. Too bad the tub wasn't
fitted with spa jets. Now *that* would have been
heaven.

Just as she was about to relax, her butt lost firm contact with the bottom of the tub. Her lower body *whooshed* forward, and a startled shriek ripped from her throat. She banged her elbow on the porcelain and grabbed for the built-in soap dish. Water sloshed over the side of the tub. The ends of her short hair got wet, but she was able to catch herself before she went completely under.

When she finally managed to stop slipping and sliding like a pod of boiled okra on a wet glass plate, she was halfway to the front of the tub, hanging on to the rim for dear life, her body twisted at an unnatural angle. The side of her knee was wedged beneath the faucet, but somehow, miraculously, she'd kept her splinted arm out of the water.

"You okay in there, sugar?"

She froze at the sound of Colby's voice coming through the closed bathroom door. Her heart slammed against her ribs and she was having a small amount of trouble catching her breath.

So, was she okay?

Well, she was naked, she'd just gone on an impromptu slip-and-slide that had made her head and her side start aching all over again, and as she clung to the side of the tub she was not altogether certain she could right herself from this awkwardly twisted, slippery position.

"Um…yes. I'm fine."

"Did you find the plastic bag?"

"Yes. Thanks." She tried not to pant. By gosh, she was exhausted.

"Good. You're not supposed to get the splint wet."

"I know that, Colby. Thank you."

For a minute all was silent.

"Are you sure you're okay? It sounded like you fell."

"No…um, I didn't fall. I'm in the tub." A body couldn't very well fall when it was already lying down.

But a person could certainly drown, she thought. Especially if that person's entire balance was off due to one arm being wrapped up to the size of Godzilla's thigh!

Lord above, that doc must have used five rolls of stretch bandage over the stiff-as-steel splint.

"How about I just stay right here at the door in case you need me," Colby said.

"No, really. You go on. I'm just about finished, anyway. Besides, I'm left-handed. So this isn't as much of a bother as you might think." *Liar, liar, pants on fire.*

Knowing that Colby was wandering freely through her bedroom was a bit disconcerting. She held still for a few seconds, until she was fairly certain that he no longer had his ear pressed to the door, ready to burst in at a moment's notice. Carefully, she used her knees and her good arm to lever herself into a sitting position, then hung her injured arm over the side of the tub.

Okay, this was way too much fun. Deciding she'd had about all the relaxing soaking she could stand for one day, she opened the drain to let out the water and climbed out of the tub, nearly pulling down the shower curtain in her efforts to gain solid footing.

She soon found that pampering the right side of her body wasn't too much of a hardship, but the left side was a huge problem. She managed to get lotion smoothed into most of her skin—all except her left arm and hand. By the time she finished, she was sweating and felt as though she needed another bath.

With the towel wrapped around her, she peeked out the bathroom door, making sure Colby wasn't sitting in wait at the foot of the bed or something.

The coast was clear, so she darted over and locked the bedroom door. She'd wrestled enough with herself in the bathroom to admit that getting dressed wasn't going to be an easy task, and she didn't want Colby walking in on her in the middle of it all.

Since she hadn't done laundry in over a week, her choice of splint-friendly clothes was at a minimum. She sifted through the hangers in her closet and decided on a summer skirt because it had an elastic waist and she could step right into it. Plus, she'd bought a cute copper top and matching sandals that she hadn't worn yet, and they'd go perfectly with the long, sand-colored, tiered skirt.

She pinched open the clothespin-type hanger, and the skirt dropped to the floor of her closet. Dragging it out with her toes, she left it puddled in the middle of the floor and extracted a pair of bikini underwear from the dresser drawer.

Despite there being very little material to the

underwear, the panties were rolled into a twisted wad by the time she got them past her thighs— one-handed. She had to sit on the end of the bed and catch her breath before she could continue.

Clearly she should have dried off better or used some talcum powder. It was too late for those measures because the nylon and lace triangles were already wound up like a fat rubber band.

By the time she finally got the panties in place she was breathing hard. Maybe she ought to rethink that aerobics class that Drucilla Taggat kept trying to get her to sign up for over at the seniors center. She hadn't realized how pitifully inadequate her stamina was.

Dreading the process, she stepped into her skirt, then proceeded to tug, pull and shimmy until she had it up around her waist.

Shaking her bangs out of her eyes, she stared at herself in the dresser mirror and faced the next dilemma—managing the hooks on her bra. It was a back closure design and she had a hard enough time getting the stupid thing on with two good hands. One-handed was going to be a joke. Of course, she could always give the girls a day off and go braless. She wasn't all that well endowed, anyway. A 32-B if it was padded. An A if it wasn't. Pitiful.

She got up and slid the short-sleeved, copper-colored top off the hanger, holding it up to the light. Too thin to skip the bra. The fabric was a stretch, polyester-and-rayon that was incredibly soft to the touch.

And would be incredibly clingy to the nipples.

But the fabric had enough give to get the bulky splint through the armhole. Becca sighed. Laundry was definitely going to be moved to the top of her to-do list. She threaded her arms through the bra straps, then pulled the shirt over her head and wrestled with the material until she *finally* managed to get her arms through the sleeves.

A scream of frustration built in her throat and escaped in a low moan.

The cups of her bra clung to the clingy material of her top instead of her breasts. Talk about uncomfortable.

She shoved her bangs out of her eyes. She'd been so sure she could do this on her own.

She couldn't put it off any longer—she needed help.

By dog, this was just too much. She was hot and hurting and seriously considering climbing back into bed.

The last thing she wanted to do was open that bedroom door and ask Colby Flynn to bring his sexy hands in here to fasten the hooks on her bra!

Chapter Five

Becca took a fortifying breath and adjusted the cups of her bra over her breasts as best she could. Holding it in place with her free hand, she left the bedroom and headed toward the kitchen.

She didn't make it that far. Colby was sitting on the edge of the couch in the living room, the newspaper spread on the coffee table in front of him. He looked up and she froze.

A sense of déjà vu swept over her.

For a moment, it was as though all the years and differences between them never were. How many times had she seen him in just that pose? With that exact same welcome and flirty amusement in his hazel eyes?

"You plannin' on going to town, sugar?"

She jolted and frowned.

"You're mighty dressed up for someone who's supposed to be staying in bed," he clarified.

"I've been in bed. Now I have work to do."

"I happen to be in a good position to know that your store is sometimes closed on Mondays."

"This isn't one of those Mondays."

"Stubborn woman. You having chest pains?"

"What?" Granted, she'd been knocked in the head, but she shouldn't be having this much trouble keeping up.

"You're clutching your breasts."

"Oh." She glanced down, then back up, mentally cursing the heat climbing into her cheeks. "I can't hook my bra."

"Ah."

The faint trace of amusement in his voice was just enough to annoy her. She lifted her chin. "Would you mind giving me a hand?"

"Hell, no. It'd be my pleasure."

"Don't get carried away, Flynn."

Grinning, he stepped behind her and slid his hands under her top.

She sucked in a breath and clamped her arm tighter across her breasts, trying to hold the bra cups in place.

"Mmm," he murmured close to her ear. "You smell good. Expensive. Like the perfumed air of a posh day spa."

She told herself *not* to respond to his whisky-smooth Texas drawl, yet chills raced up her spine and gooseflesh raised the hairs on her arms. "How would you know what the inside of a day spa smells like?"

"Now, now, sugar pie. Don't be sexist. Spas aren't just for you ladies."

"So you've been to one?"

"Not as a customer," he admitted, a smile in his voice. "I had a client who owned a spa. They offered all kinds of fancy services. One of the operators burned a customer during a laser treatment."

"Oh, ouch."

"It wasn't a burn like you're probably thinking. Her skin turned a bit red—which went away with no lasting effects. The customer sued, anyway, and I represented the spa's owner and the facial gal who'd done the treatment."

"Did you win?"

"Of course."

Finally, he pulled the ends of her bra together. She sucked in a breath when the band cut into her tender ribs.

"Sorry. Too tight?"

"My side's pretty sore."

"Then why wear this thing?" He released the tension so suddenly she had to make a mad grab to keep the bra cups in place.

"I'm not going to parade around without my underwear."

"You're not wearing underpants, either?"

"Yes, I'm wearing—I meant the bra!" She glanced back over her shoulder and noted that he was staring at her skirt.

"Whew. 'Bout gave me a heart attack."

"Would you just hook the damn thing?"

"No." He crossed his arms over his chest. "It'll hurt you."

"Not if you don't jerk and yank like you're

cinching the saddle on a horse, for crying out loud. Just put it on the loosest hook and it'll be fine."

He uncrossed his arms and huffed out an exasperated sigh. This time, he gently tugged the ends together. "I don't know why you won't just leave it off. You don't need it."

"Gee, thanks. I just love it when a man points out that I'm flat-chested."

"I didn't say that, sugar. You know how I feel about your—"

"Never mind!" She cut him off before he could complete the sentence, before he uttered the words he'd always said to her in the past when she'd worried that her boobs were too little. *They're the perfect size for that sexy, compact body, darlin'. Besides, more than a handful is a waste.*

"It just seems to me you're plenty uncomfortable without adding to it." He shrugged, lightly touched her side, then pulled the back of her stretchy top down to her waist. "Where's the sling?"

"On the bed."

He turned her by the shoulders and walked her the few steps back to her bedroom. Retrieving the blue apparatus from where it lay on the rumpled bedspread, he slid it over her head, carefully maneuvering her arm into place.

"Thanks," she said. "I can take it from here."

For a long moment he looked into her eyes, his expression unreadable, his gaze searching, probing, asking questions she didn't understand and wouldn't know how to answer. When he stepped back, she literally swayed, so mesmerized by him that when the contact was broken she lost her balance and nearly fell.

He steadied her, his hands lingering. "I've got the coffeepot on."

She nodded. "I'll be right there."

"You really should stay in bed with your arm propped up."

"We're not going through that again, Colby. I have work to do and customers to tend to. I appreciate your help and all, but you don't know how to run my business."

"It'll keep, sugar. Folks in this town are your friends. They'll understand."

"I need to be busy. And I need to see for myself if anything's missing. Someone was prowling through my things last night. It makes me feel violated. I've got to go back down there and get rid of any bad vibes that might be lingering. Reestablish my territory."

"Ah. You're gonna go pee on the merchandise."

She laughed and gripped her side. "I'll try not to be that crass."

"Hey. Be as crass as you want. I promise to be a spectator only."

"Yeah, right. Get out of here so I can finish dressing."

"I thought I just helped you do that."

"Do you want to apply my mascara and lipstick?"

"If you need me to, sugar, I'm all yours."

She hoped like crazy that her smile hadn't

slipped. Because an irrational part of her wanted to take his "all yours" comment literally. And that wasn't possible. Aside from the fact that they'd once tried and failed at a relationship, the man was moving halfway across the state.

"Git!" she said.

He backed toward the door. "Yes, ma'am."

Becca decided against the mascara and settled for a little blush and lip gloss. A bruise was spreading out from beneath the bandage on her forehead. Nothing she could do about that. She ran a brush through her short hair, and noted that the chunky maroon highlights hadn't faded and still contrasted nicely with her jet-black natural color.

At last she made her way to the kitchen, then stopped dead in her tracks, stunned to find it so…so spotless.

Dish soap and sponges, usually sitting out on the countertop within reach, were nowhere in sight. Her stainless-steel, industrial-size mixer was gone, as was the toaster, the electric can opener and the vacuum-pack food sealer. The only thing displayed on the white-tile surface was a set of blue-and-white china canisters, the coffeemaker and a bamboo plant in a fluted vase that matched the canister set.

For a minute she thought the burglars had hit the kitchen, as well as the store.

"Where's all my stuff?" she asked, dragging her gaze to Colby's.

"What stuff?" He whipped the dish towel over his shoulder, letting it drape there like a burp diaper.

"My appliances, for one."

"Oh. In the cupboard."

"Why?"

A smart man would have recognized her tone. Clearly, Colby had been away from her for too long because he actually looked pleased with himself.

"You're not using them. I figured they may as well be put away." From an overhead cabinet, he got out a cup and saucer.

"I don't put them away because I *do* use them. Often. It's a much bigger hassle to have to stoop over and drag them out of cupboards several times a day."

"That often, hmm?"

"This kitchen's not just for show, Colby. I actually cook and bake in it." She glanced around, wondered what other damage he'd done.

Every surface she spied practically had a mirror shine. The unused magnets on her refrigerator door were relocated to the side of the appliance and organized by size and shape. All of the baby photographs of Chelsa and Amanda were lined up in a perfect square, edges touching as though aligned by a ruler. Scraps of paper, notes, recipes and knitting patterns she'd cut out of magazines and tacked to the face of the fridge with ladybug magnets were missing.

The fact that he'd been touching the refrigerator at all gave her a very bad feeling.

Slowly, she crossed the room, and pulled open the door of the white, side-by-side fridge.

Her stomach dropped clear to her toes. The blood

in her veins pulsed faster, setting up a throb in her injured head.

"What have you done with Maizy?" Her voice rose, despite her intention to stay calm and give him the benefit of the doubt.

She wouldn't get overwrought. She simply wouldn't.

She would *not* kill Colby Flynn.

"Who's Maizy?" he asked, reaching past her to retrieve the carton of half-and-half and a plate of cantaloupe.

"My sourdough starter. I had her in a fruit jar. The one with little cherries around the rim?"

"I washed a jar with cherries on it. It had some foul-smelling goop inside."

"Oh, no! You didn't! Please tell me you didn't throw away my starter."

"If it was in that cherry jar, I did. It was rancid. God knows how long it's been there."

"Yes, God knows and so do I," she said. "It's been in there since Grandma Lee gave it to me ten years ago! My Sunday school teacher gave it to Grandma Lee twenty years before that! And it wasn't foul-smelling *or* rancid."

He looked genuinely perplexed. "What the devil is a *starter,* anyway? And why would you save something for ten years in your refrigerator?"

"I use it to make breads. You feed it, and add different ingredients—"

"*Feed* it?"

"—to it. Yes. Feed it. Naturally, I have to use

some of it to make my bread and that portion needs to be replaced. You feed it to keep it alive and plentiful. Unless you mistreat it, it'll last for countless years."

"Well, doggone, sugar. I guess I mistreated it big time, because I *fed* it to the garbage disposal." He poured her a cup of coffee, added a dash of cream, stirred and brought the cup to her. "Will you accept a peace offering?"

He closed the refrigerator door, then held out the cup and saucer. The china pattern was Old Country Roses. One of her favorites.

Her eyes watered and a lump formed in her aching throat. She felt as though she'd lost a final piece of Grandma Lee's life.

And she felt stupid for getting weepy.

When she didn't take the coffee from him, he bent his knees to peer into her face. "Oh, man."

He slid the cup and saucer onto the table and pulled her close. "I made you cry. I'm sorry, Becca Sue. I didn't mean to be flip."

She looked up, met the sincerity in his hazel eyes. How could she be upset with him? He was only trying to help.

He'd rescued her from a burglar, given up his time to take her to the hospital, offered to make her *soup,* for goodness sake. He'd watched over her like a concerned rooster—a very sexy rooster—and from the looks of her spotless apartment, he'd been very busy on her behalf.

Misguided, but sweet nonetheless.

And he'd remembered that she took cream with her coffee.

She blinked and stepped back, determined to get a grip.

"I'm not crying. And I'll accept your apology and peace offering on one condition. You have to promise me that starting now—and from this day forward—you'll leave my refrigerator *and* its contents alone."

He drew in a breath. Clearly, this was difficult for him. He couldn't seem to help himself from organizing. "Yeah, I'll leave all the stinky spongy stuff alone."

"*And* the appliances."

"We'll see."

"Colby…"

"I'll make a deal with you. When you're back up to snuff and are using the appliances on your own, I'll try to leave them alone. But as long as I'm chief cook in the kitchen, they stay in the cupboard."

"Who said you were going to be chief cook in the kitchen?"

"I did. And the doc. And Lily will probably say the same when we go in Friday for a follow-up check on your hand." Lily O'Rourke was Becca's primary doctor. She ran her own practice out of the clinic, but didn't put in the late hours that the emergency doctors did, nor did she work weekends. She'd paid her dues, she said.

Becca reached for her cup and took a sip of coffee. It was good. "Colby, you don't have to stay here or cook and clean for me. I can manage."

"Too late. You already accepted my peace offering."

"I did not."

"The coffee?" He nodded to her cup. "You drank. That's a binding contract. Like a gentleman's agreement."

"Your peace offering was an apology for killing Maizy. It had nothing to do with anything else."

"Yes, it did—it had to do with cleaning. And that involves the appliances. And while I'm staying here, they can live in the cupboards."

Becca dropped her forehead into her palm, then winced. Despite the slight sting, she managed a chuckle. "Is this how you win your law cases? Talk in circles until you get your opponent so confused they just give in?"

He grinned at her and winked.

Her stomach did a cartwheel.

"I'm very good at my chosen profession," he said.

"Yes, well, you be sure and concentrate on what you do best and let me handle my own domain."

"Your domain could use a bit of help, sugar."

She shook her head. "You might have spent the night here, but we don't live together anymore. That means I'm allowed to be as messy as I want. You can't break up with me twice because we're total opposites."

He stared at her for a long moment, then said quietly, seriously, "That's not why we broke up, Becca."

"Maybe not." She shrugged, uncomfortable with his direct stare. "But it's a reminder. We drove each other crazy." Why in the world had she brought up this subject?

"In some ways, it was a very good kind of crazy."

In bed, he meant. Flustered, she set her cup in the sink. "I need to put some rolls in the oven."

He blocked her way. "That part was good, wasn't it?"

"This conversation is inappropriate."

"Wasn't it?" he persisted.

"You know it was. But sex can't be the only thing holding a relationship together. I still want a family. You're moving to Dallas to chase your dream. There's a mighty wide gap between your wants and mine." She raised an eyebrow, daring him to argue.

The gesture made her forehead hurt.

The unreadable emotion in his hazel eyes made her heart ache.

She took a breath. "Maybe it's not such a good idea for you to hang out here, Colby."

"Doesn't look like you're in any shape to get rid of me." A muscle tightened in his jaw, a sure sign that he was annoyed and holding back.

"Why are you doing this?"

"Hell if I know. I told you I'd get you pregnant when you turned thirty if no other man had snapped you up! Ever since your birthday, that's all I can think about."

A shocked silence filled the kitchen.

Well, how about that? At least she had her answer. He *did* remember.

Which made them *both* a couple of fools.

She needed to lighten the mood. Quickly. Cut through the tension. Run as far away from this conversation as possible.

"Um…" She cleared her throat. "I believe we were pretty drunk when you made that promise, so don't give it another thought. You're off the hook. Besides—" she pointed to her sling "—I'm also not in the best of shape to…um, do what it takes to get pregnant. And by the time I am, you'll be gone. So. Subject closed." *Shut up, Becca Sue.* Lordy. That lick on the head had obviously given her diarrhea of the mouth. "Would you mind getting those rolls out of the fridge? I'll preheat the oven." *And pray for a hole to appear in the floor and swallow me up.*

"Just like that?" he asked. "Conversation's over?"

She twisted the temperature dial on the oven and noted that her hand was shaking. "Yep. My house. My rules."

He was silent behind her, and she didn't dare turn around to look at him. She wasn't sure how much more of these up-and-down emotions she could take. As it was, she was about to drop in her tracks, and it wasn't even 8:00 a.m.

"Becca?" His hand suddenly appeared, covering hers over the temperature dial on the oven. "Come sit down before you fall."

He twisted the oven knob to the "off" position, steered her to the kitchen table, seated her, then grabbed another chair and turned it around. Straddling it, he crossed his arms over the top of the wooden back.

"About those rules," he began. "I think we should work out a reasonable compromise. No sense in us butting heads when all I want to do is help out. We're friends. We used to be more, but I think we can get past that if we try. You've had someone break into your store and we don't yet know what he was after, or if he'll be back."

Her heart jumped into her throat. "Why would you think he'll come back?"

"How long have you lived here?" It was a rhetorical question. "Have you ever known any of the businesses on Main Street to get broken into—other than Chandler's drugstore when that group of kids on a scavenger hunt helped themselves to a few tubes of hemorrhoid cream."

She would have smiled at the memory, but the point he was making made her shiver. "I guess not."

"Exactly. And whoever was in here was interrupted. First by you, and then by me. Who knows what he was after. Call me jaded, but I can't get my mind wrapped around this being a random break-in."

"Are you deliberately trying to scare me so I'll let you play the White Knight? Because I might be in a little distress here—" she gestured to her sling "—but I can assure you I'm no damsel—"

He placed a finger over her lips, stopping her words. "I know. You're a firecracker. All five-foot-three-inches of you."

She opened her mouth to object, but he pressed on.

"I've never been anyone's White Knight, sugar—

don't intend to be, for that matter. But I don't mind being a friend. Let me help you out here. At least for my own peace of mind."

Darn it. He was the only man she knew who could turn her insides to jelly with a mere shift of tone. And whether he wanted to admit it or not, he'd definitely been her hero last night, rushing to her rescue and scaring off the bad guy.

"If you make me leave, I won't get a wink of sleep worrying about you being over here on your own with a madman burglar on the loose."

"Okay, okay. Now you're stretching it." She laughed. She couldn't help it. Yes, they'd had a relationship in the past. And, yes, there was still a sexual spark between them—a really *hot* sexual spark. But facts were facts. She needed help and he was offering.

They were adults. Despite his sexual innuendos, she knew that he was a man who wanted no strings attached—she could accept that. And that he was leaving town in three weeks proved he hadn't changed his mind.

Oh, she'd fantasized a lot over the past year, convinced herself that perhaps *she* was the reason he'd returned to Hope Valley, allowed herself to read more into the fact that the only women he hung out with on occasion were her and her friends.

Wishful thinking.

"What about your law practice?" she asked. "If you're going to keep house for me and mind my store, who's going to take care of your business?"

"Most all my cases are wrapped up. I'm pretty

much on vacation, taking some time packing up. I'll forward my business phone to my cell, and I can handle any loose ends from over here."

"Sounds like you've got it all figured out."

"Sounds like." He waited for her answer. They both knew he'd leave if she really wanted him to.

"All right. I'd shake on it, but my hand's a bit useless at the moment. And thank you. I appreciate the help."

He stood. "No problem."

"Now that I think about it, I just may like having a man at my beck and call. Turn the oven back on to 350 degrees and grab those rolls out of the fridge."

"Uh-uh." He shook his head. "You've got enough stuff here to get us through the day." He indicated the covered platter of cinnamon rolls and the loaf of zucchini bread he'd already removed from the freezer. "So, you want one of these cinnamon rolls for breakfast, or toast and eggs?"

She could tell by the way he was eyeing the rolls what his choice was. "No sense dragging the toaster out of hiding when we've got *almost* fresh-baked rolls in front of us."

"My thoughts exactly." He plucked two rolls and popped them into the microwave, forked some cantaloupe slices into fruit bowls, then fished a pain pill out of the sack the hospital had sent home with them and set it by her plate.

"I really should bake that other batch of cinnamon rolls that are in the fridge," she said. "Especially since we're eating part of the merchandise here."

Again, he shook his head. "Best to ration what we have. Especially since I killed old stinkpot Maizy."

Chapter Six

After he'd cleaned up the breakfast dishes, Colby opened the stairwell door. The narrow passageway wouldn't allow for them to go side-by-side, so he went first. If she lost her footing or got woozy, he'd at least break her fall.

Stubborn woman. She ought to be in bed, as the doc told her. Okay, he didn't actually tell her to stay in bed. Just to rest.

Colby didn't think Becca Sue Ellsworth knew the meaning of the word *rest*.

He noticed that Trouble had already used his kitty doors at the top and bottom of the stairwell and was sitting in the store window, leisurely licking his paws. The cat looked around as they entered, then went back to his bathing.

"It looks like hardly anything in here has been touched," Becca said, stopping to look around. "Who cleaned up all the black dust?"

"I did. Had some trouble sleeping last night."

Colby crossed to the glass bakery case and set the plate of rolls on top of it.

"I'm sorry. Usually, that couch is pretty comfortable."

"The couch was fine. It was my mind that wouldn't settle down." Most of Becca's furniture was Victorian in design—not the little bitty dainty kind, but the type with high arms and backs and plenty of padding. On just about every surface, knitted and crocheted afghans were draped, inviting company to curl up and get comfortable.

Her shop was pretty much the same. There were bistro tables and chairs for drinking coffee or eating sweets, overstuffed armchairs for relaxing and reading. She'd designed the place for socializing, as well as for making a living.

A nice touch.

The minute he turned his back, Becca bent over to put the rolls and zucchini bread into the sealed glass case. Even though she'd spread the cinnamon rolls out in a staggered pattern, the pastry case still looked like a picked-over table at a church social.

He saw her sway slightly and he swore. Colby swept an arm around her waist and maneuvered her onto a stool.

"I need to start the coffee," she protested.

"It's already made and in the carafe. Now you just sit and point your finger. I'll do any work that needs doing."

"I won't be manhandled, Colby. And I can't very

well take inventory to see if anything's missing if I'm sitting on a chair."

"I'm trying to help out, Becca Sue. And you're pale as a sheet. Despite the poor example my folks set, I pride myself on being chivalrous around the ladies. You're turning that gentlemanly virtue into a major frustration."

A dimple winked in her smooth cheek when she laughed at him. "My apologies, kind sir. I didn't mean to step on your ego."

"Right. Pull the other leg, sugar."

"Did you sleep at *all* last night?"

"Some." *None.* Maybe half an hour, he thought. But *he* hadn't been attacked by an intruder. He could deal with a little lost sleep. Becca couldn't.

And it annoyed him that she wouldn't do what he wanted her to do. Short of hauling her back up those stairs, there wasn't much he could do about her determination to be up and around.

Almost before they'd unlocked the door and flipped over the "open" sign, Millicent Lloyd came in carrying a platter filled with chocolate chip cookies, lemon bars and fudge.

"Ah," Colby said. "A woman after my own heart." He took the goodies out of her hands and astonished the small elderly woman with a kiss on her powdered cheek.

"I heard about your injuries," Millicent said to Becca while eyeing Colby suspiciously. "Can't imagine what this world's comin' to. Break-ins on Main Street. Humph. Figured you'd need some help with the baked goods. And I brought the medication the doc prescribed for you, too."

"You didn't have to do that, Millie."

"Oh, pshaw. I was in Chandler's picking up some cold cream, anyway. Figured I might as well save you a trip." She sniffed, waved her gloved hand as though her good deed was no big deal. Millicent Lloyd wore gloves year round, the season and date determining their color. Today, they were a buttery tan to match her shoes and her pocketbook.

"Thank you," Becca said. "That was sweet. How much do I owe you?"

"Not a dime, that's for sure. You don't think I'd let that old coot charge you for a few measly pills, do you? Blasted drug companies act like they own the world. Paddin' the pockets of half the doctors and pharmacists around. I let Chandler know right quick he wasn't getting away with gouging you after you'd been through such a trauma. And that was that. Handed 'em over for free, he did, and sent along his best wishes for a speedy recovery to boot."

Colby could tell that Becca wanted to smile, but knew better. Millicent Lloyd was an eccentric old lady whose hair was a subtle shade of gray-blue. Donetta had finally gotten her to tone it down, but couldn't convince the woman to get rid of the color completely. Colby had heard the girls talking about it over at Anna's Café. Millicent claimed that her late husband, Harold, loved it blue and she was keeping it that way in his honor. She was gruff and opinionated. Half the town was scared of her and the other half gossiped about her. And just recently, they'd found out that she owned most of the buildings on Main Street—which made her Becca's landlady.

But Millicent Lloyd had a heart of gold, and behind the gruff was pure marshmallow.

Colby arranged the cookies and fudge in the glass case and figured he'd be half broke and five pounds heavier by the end of the day. All these sweets were way too much temptation.

He was heartily grateful to Miz Lloyd, though. Her contribution gave him another day without having to bake. He hadn't realized how nervous he was over that aspect of helping Becca. He didn't like to do something unless he was fairly certain he could do it perfectly—or at least above adequately. Baking might be more of a challenge than he was prepared for.

At least, following in Becca's culinary footsteps would be. Her scones, breads and cinnamon rolls were to-die-for delicious and sinful. Which was why he made it a point to limit himself—both to seeing Becca Sue and to tasting her delicacies. Baked ones, he reminded himself when his mind wanted to go elsewhere.

"I'll take one of them cinnamon rolls while you're in there," Millicent said, nodding toward the glass case. She tugged off her cotton gloves and folded them into her pocketbook.

Colby grabbed a pair of tongs and snagged a roll, then looked around for something to put it on.

"The plates are behind you in the cabinet." Becca pointed with her free hand.

"Just wrap it up to go," Millicent said. "I've a few stops to make yet this morning." She withdrew her wallet.

"Put away your money," Becca said. "You're not paying for that cinnamon roll."

"Of course I am. What kind of businesswoman are you, anyway? You don't just go around givin' away the merchandise."

"You *brought* the merchandise."

"I brought cookies and fudge. I'm *buying* a cinnamon roll." She held out two crisp, one-dollar bills, her body language and expression insisting she'd hear no arguments from either of them.

With an apologetic look in Becca's direction, Colby accepted the money, then stared at the cash register, not sure how to record the sale or open the cash drawer. He was going to need a quick seminar in retail sales.

Knowing from past experience that Becca charged a dollar and fifty cents for the rolls, he reached in his pocket and pulled out two quarters, handing them over to Miz Lloyd.

Millicent raised an eyebrow and accepted the coins. "You be sure and reconcile this transaction, young man. I appreciate that you're helping out our Becca, but she won't thank you for ruining her bookkeeping."

"Yes, ma'am."

"And you make sure she rests."

"I intend to, ma'am. Just as soon as I get a few pointers on how everything works."

"In case the two of you have forgotten," Becca interrupted, "I'm sitting right here."

Millicent patted Becca's good arm, gave it a gentle squeeze. "Of course you are, dear. But you shouldn't be. I'll come back by and check on you later in the day—just to make sure this rounder hasn't given away half the store or run you into the ground. If need be, I can manage to wait on customers."

Becca smiled. "We'll be fine, Millie."

The older woman sniffed. "That remains to be seen." She tugged on her gloves, gathered up her cinnamon roll and her empty platter and left the store.

"Well," Colby said. "Our first customer."

"Yes, and you're already fifty cents out of pocket." She slid off the stool and pulled it closer to the cash register. "I'll show you how this works. The register at the front counter is the same model. It's just easier to keep the two sides of the shop separate. I use this one for food and drink items, and the front machine for retail purchases."

He wrote down the instructions as she showed him, making a cheat sheet that he could keep beside the cash register…because as soon as he felt halfway capable of running the store on his own, he was going to insist that she go back to bed—even if he had to carry her there.

He could see the lines of tension on her face as she perused the shelves in search of missing merchandise, noted the paleness of her skin when she leaned forward to rearrange the rack of books he'd righted. Obviously he hadn't gotten the books back into their proper slots. She was in pain but too mule-headed to admit it. Miss Independent.

As it turned out, he didn't have to do any insisting or resort to he-man tactics. By midmorning, the pain medication had obviously kicked in. While he was brewing another pot of coffee, he saw her sink into the overstuffed chair she kept by a rack of books so customers could sit and read if they chose, and the next thing he knew, her legs were curled beneath her and she was sound asleep.

He picked up a lightweight afghan and draped it over her. He wanted to prop a pillow under her sling to elevate her arm, but didn't want to chance waking her. Becca Sue was as stubborn as all get out, and it was exasperating trying to stay one step ahead of her.

For a long moment, he watched her sleep, her short, black hair with its chunky maroon highlights feathering across her cheek. She'd always been daring when it came to her hair or her clothes, not afraid to try out a new look or style. But he wouldn't call her trendy—at least not in the sense that she followed trends. If anything, she was the one who started them. If the look caught on, she'd change hers, not wanting to be part of the crowd.

She definitely stood out. Her green eyes were a striking contrast to her dark hair and olive complexion. Small and compact, she was gorgeous. At one time, he'd had the right to know every inch of that sweet body. And even after seven years, he hadn't forgotten a single detail.

Although he still lusted after her, had, in fact, never stopped, they'd managed to remain friends over the years. He was grateful for that, because he couldn't imagine a life without her in it.

One of these days, she would have her home and hearth and babies that she wanted so badly—the family life he still didn't see as part of his own future. When that day came, he wondered how he would handle seeing her with another man, watching that dimple in her cheek when she smiled at another guy.

Because when Becca Sue smiled at you, it made you feel ten feet tall. She put her whole self into her smile and was the most genuine person he knew.

He was going to miss that when he left.

The bell above the front door jingled. He looked up and saw that the customer was Tracy Lynn, carrying her baby daughter wrapped in a pink blanket. Probably knitted by Becca Sue, he thought.

He put his finger to his lips, and Tracy Lynn nodded.

They moved across the store and stood next to one of the bistro tables.

"Can I get you something?" Colby asked, taking a peek at the tiny baby in her arms.

"No. I just came to check on Becca, see if she needed anything."

"She's stubborn as a mule. It's damn hard to do anything for the woman. Her idea of accepting help is to let you tag along beside her as she works herself to the bone."

Tracy Lynn smiled. "You don't have to convince me."

Of course, he thought. Becca, Tracy Lynn, Sunny and Donetta had been a tight foursome since grade school, maybe even longer. Her three friends knew Becca Sue inside and out. He'd lived with her for only a few months one summer, loved her, then they'd been apart for a long time.

"Chelsa has an appointment with the pediatrician this morning," Tracy Lynn said, "but I can come back afterward if Becca needs help here."

Colby shook his head. "I think I've got it covered."

"I just can't believe this happened. Was anything stolen?"

Before he could answer, Donetta, carrying her infant daughter, and Sunny, pregnant and looking about to pop, came through the door. Storm Carmichael, dressed in his sheriff's uniform today, followed the women inside. Both Colby and Tracy Lynn put silencing fingers to their lips and pointed toward Becca sleeping in the chair.

Colby shouldn't be so relieved that these folks were friends rather than actual customers. But he was. He still felt a bit out of his element minding the store on his own.

"We should probably prop a pillow under her head and arm," Sunny said, resting her hand on her swollen stomach.

"I don't want to wake her," Colby said.

"Are you kidding?" Donetta gave a soft laugh. "Once she's out, Becca Sue sleeps like the dead."

Why hadn't he known that about her?

"At a sleepover one time," Tracy Lynn added, "we trickled water on her head and all she did was roll over and snuggle further under the blankets."

Donetta passed her baby to Storm.

Tracy Lynn turned to Colby and said, "Here."

The next thing Colby knew his arms were filled with a warm, sleeping baby swaddled in a fluffy knitted blanket. The switch was handled so quickly he didn't have time to object. God Almighty, he'd never held a baby in his life. He froze like a wooden statue, not sure where to focus his attention, scared to death he was going to drop this kid and break her.

"Relax," Storm said, coming to stand next to him. "Babies are sturdier than they look."

"That's your opinion. Besides, you've had some practice."

Colby watched as the girls went into action. There were throw pillows in various places around the store, most with embroidered slogans on them having to do with the merits of friendship and cat ownership. Donetta, Tracy Lynn and Sunny gathered them up and huddled around the chair where Becca Sue was curled.

Colby held his breath. Not only because he had this smaller-than-a-flea infant in his arms, but because he was sure someone was going to wake up Becca.

With that stupid baby pact he'd made all those years ago and knowing how much Becca loved kids, he knew deep in his bones that he did not want her waking up and seeing him holding a baby. He wasn't sure why he felt so strongly about that. Or so guilty.

Don't go there, Flynn.

Okay, he didn't want her waking up and him having to argue and hassle with her to take it easy, that was all.

The bruise spreading beneath the bandage on her head still upset him. Getting her to slow down and accept help wasn't easy, and the longer she slept, the more she'd heal and the fewer arguments they'd have to endure.

Hell, he could flip the "closed" sign on the door and she wouldn't even know it. The townsfolk would understand, and any other stray customers could just come back at a more convenient time.

But he knew he wouldn't do that. She was worried about finances. He had no idea about the state of her bank account, and he didn't want to be the cause of lowering it. On the other hand, he could slip a couple of hundred bucks in the cash register and call it a day.

True to her friends' prediction, Becca didn't even stir as pillows were gently put under her arm and head, and the afghan tucked back around her.

The baby in his arms wiggled and his gut lodged right up under his ribs. He stared down at the round little face. Okay, she was pretty cute. She was sucking on her bottom lip like she was starvin' half to death. As long as she didn't start rooting around his chest, they'd get along fine.

"Did Becca Sue have a chance to check her inventory to see what's missing?" Storm asked.

Colby wasn't sure if he could talk and hold the baby at the same time. He gave it a shot.

"Near as we can tell so far, nothing was taken. Both cash registers had a hundred dollars in change in them—same amount Becca said she always keeps in them. She'd already made a bank deposit yesterday, so there wasn't any other cash lying around. She checked all the shelves and seems to think everything's here. I don't see how she can be so sure. There's little rhyme or reason to the placement of most of this stuff—and there's a whole lot of it."

Storm chuckled. "Trust me. Becca knows every inch of this store. She buys the merchandise herself, mostly from estate sales. Donetta says she considers all these various items her friends."

"Friends?"

"Yeah. They have a story to tell or something."

Weird, Colby thought. He wasn't big on family. His was a really poor example of what one should be. He had no contact with either of his parents—who were divorced—and they seemed okay with the status quo. Out of sight, out of mind. Don't care a damn. *Great background you got, Flynn.*

Just thinking about his parents made him doubly uncomfortable holding this tiny baby, and he couldn't seem to pass her back fast enough when

Tracy Lynn held out her arms. What the hell did he know about kids and how to interact with them? His own folks had barely talked to him while he was growing up. When they did, it was usually in the middle of a yelling match with each other about money—or the lack of it—when he tried to intervene and beg them to be nice to each other, and they hollered at him to stay the hell out of their business.

They'd finally divorced, and when he was fifteen—a rebellious fifteen—his mother had shipped him off to military school as if he'd been no more than a stray mutt she'd been tossing food to all those years and was sick of it.

"Skeeter's going to stop by later with a new lock for the back door," Storm said. "Can you handle installing it?"

Colby gave him a dirty look. "How soon you forget who did the lion's share of work on your wife's beauty salon to bring it up to code."

Donetta threaded her arm through her husband's and raised her eyebrows, which were the same fiery red as her hair. "Storm told me that *he* did most of the work."

"And you believed him?" Colby winked.

"Okay. I think it's time for me to go to work before you get me in a fight with my wife." Storm passed the baby to Donetta and gave both his wife and daughter a kiss. "I don't hold out much hope for fingerprints. Too many customers in and out of here. I'm still running the ones we lifted, though. Maybe we'll get lucky and something will spit out of the national database. Meanwhile, we can hope that it was just a random hit and you interrupted them before they took anything."

The other alternative, Colby knew, was that someone was looking for something in particular. One never knew what might get sold at an estate sale by mistake—and Storm had just said Becca did most of her buying at estate sales. A sane, upstanding citizen would come and negotiate with the purchaser for a return of the heirloom.

But then, there were always the dregs of society, the ones who felt the world owed them a living and wouldn't think twice about busting in and forcibly taking back what was no longer theirs. If that were the case and the scumbag had been interrupted, he'd be back.

Colby hoped he was just letting his imagination run away with him, compliments of his line of work. But until he felt a little surer and Becca Sue didn't look so defenseless, he intended to camp out here and keep a close watch.

Which was no more, he told himself, than any good friend would do. And he was the smartest choice to do so. He didn't have any family ties. He had three weeks of free time on his hands.

And if he wanted to be absolutely honest, he was looking forward to spending those three weeks with Becca Sue.

Once her friends left, Colby walked around the store, looking for clues to what a thief might want to steal and trying to familiarize himself with the store so that he didn't have to turn to Becca every two minutes to ask a question.

The place smelled of coffee, cinnamon, wood, books and spicy incense. The hardwood planks creaked beneath his feet as he walked. He imagined this was the building's original floor. The boards were worn but clean, and permeated with the various scents from sixty years of comings and goings and the multitude of items that had been stored within these walls.

There was a whole bunch of china stuff—cups and saucers, mismatched plates, teapots—scattered among other merchandise on the various shelves. Seemed to him it would make more sense to group like items together. If he were in the market for dishes, it'd make it a whole lot easier if he could just go to one shelf and pick out what he wanted and be done with it. As it was, a person would have to go on a hunt that would likely take the whole day. He figured the average person would get frustrated and just leave without making a purchase.

Clearing off some shelves between an antique-looking curio cabinet and a rack of linens and yarn, he gathered up some of the china, freezing for a moment when the glass pieces rattled against each other. Becca didn't stir. Okay, he needn't tiptoe. He set about organizing the china, having to search all over the store for the different glassware items that were tucked in among all the other trinkets and junk on the shelves. Then he tackled the candles and scented stuff she had stashed willy-nilly.

After a half hour of sniffing each candle and bag of potpourri so he could group them by scent, he'd developed a headache.

It was a wonder he accomplished anything at all.

Half the townsfolk came in during the morning to take a peek at Becca, get the skinny on what had happened, and then for some reason, the majority of them glared at him in warning, as if he were the wolf paying a call on Little Red Riding Hood. He didn't get it.

Almost everyone who came through the doors bought something, though, and he was especially proud that he'd sold a pitcher with an oversize handle that looked like an angel's wing for three hundred bucks. At first he'd thought the price tag was wrong. But Mrs. Norah Conway had whipped out her American Express card without batting an eyelash.

Not bad for a morning's work, he thought, glancing over at Becca to make sure she was still asleep. He wouldn't have to pad the till, after all.

And with the sandwiches and casserole that Anna Carmichael had dropped off, he wouldn't have to cook, either. Things were moving along just fine, he thought.

In his law practice, he was in the business of helping people out of a jam. He figured he was pretty much doing the same for Becca Sue.

He was surprised that this type of shop did so well in a small town. Not being in the retail business himself, he hadn't realized how many out-of-town customers dropped in and how many locals depended on Becca Sue to have just the right gift.

When his cell phone rang, his gaze whipped to Becca Sue, then to the caller ID. *Wells and Steadman.*

He punched the button and moved across the room so he wouldn't disturb her. At least that's what he told himself. No reason to feel guilty about making plans to change jobs and move to another city.

"Colby Flynn," he answered.

"Mornin', Colby. Steven Wells, here. How's it going on your end?"

"The sun's shining. Couldn't be better."

Steven boomed a laugh. "That's what I like about you, boy. Always optimistic. Listen, we've got us a big case brewing. Oil company's being raked over the coals by the EPA. Big dollars are at stake. This is just the sort of thing to make a name for the attorneys who handle it, and I wanted to make sure you got in on it. You interested in second chair?"

Dumb question. He could already feel his saliva glands flowing. "How soon's the hearing?"

"A couple months out yet, but there's a lot of preparing to do."

"Think it'll to go trial?"

"Yes. It'll be a tough one, but representing oil companies in this kind of litigation is our specialty. Thought I'd fax over the preliminaries for you to have a look-see—unless you can move up your time frame for relocating? In that case, you can pore over the whole file right here in your private office. I've already had your name painted on the door. Cassandra's picked out the carpet and furnishings. Should be all set for you by Friday."

Friday was the day Becca was due back at the doctor's office.

Colby hesitated and glanced over his shoulder at Becca. He saw her stirring.

He had no qualms about allowing Steven's daughter, Cassandra, free rein decorating his office. She was classy, had been born and bred into the corporate world. She didn't have a single frilly gene in her, plus, she had champagne tastes and the finest vintage Cristal pocketbook to go with it.

He glanced around at the scarred hardwood floors and crammed display shelves, the powder-blue knitted baby blanket lying atop a spindly legged table, a wooden rooster serving as a bookend. Cassandra wouldn't know what to do with herself in a shop like this. She was into modern furnishings, fine art and expensive gems—not antiques, collectibles or costume jewelry.

Colby thought about his bulletin board with the lawyer jokes pinned to it. Definitely not going to blend with his new office decor at Wells, Steadman and Flynn.

As for speeding up his moving date, Colby felt an uncharacteristic reluctance. Odd, because he'd really been looking forward to the change, the challenge.

"Friday's a bit soon for me, Steven. I've still got

a couple of obligations and loose ends here to tie up. Why don't you go ahead and fax the paperwork? That'll at least give me a head start."

"No problem. Any idea when you'll be here for good? I know you said you were going to take a bit of a vacation, but this case is a pretty big deal."

"I shouldn't have too much trouble getting up to speed. You having second thoughts about my qualifications, Steven?"

Wells laughed. "Not a one. To tell the truth, Cassandra's been hounding me some. Just thought I could give her an update."

Colby nodded. "Tell her we're still pretty much looking at three weeks."

"Will do. Take care, son. See you soon."

Colby flipped closed the cell phone and stood there for a moment. This kind of high-paying job was exactly what he'd wanted ever since he was a sullen fifteen-year-old in military school.

He'd gone head-to-fist with just about everyone at school in those first few months, taken some hard knocks, but he'd finally accepted his plight and settled in, and had decided he'd one day make something of himself. He'd have money and a fine house and the most expensive car.

So, okay, he had those things now. Maybe not the most expensive house and car, but at least they were the ones he'd chosen, the ones he could easily afford.

He made a very good living in his private practice here in Hope Valley, mostly because many of his clients were from Austin. But he would make a super-wealthy living with Wells and Steadman. And for the kid inside him—the one who'd been made to feel as though he were little better than a stray dog—that was a mighty big draw.

"Why'd you let me sleep so long?" Becca asked, coming up behind him.

He turned and smiled at the way her hair stuck up on the side. "You need the rest."

"Hmm. You're sure pillow happy. I didn't even feel you stuff them around me."

"That was Sunny, Tracy and Donetta's doings."

"They were here? Why didn't you wake me?"

"Wasn't on my to-do list." He winked at her and gave in to the temptation to smooth down the stray lock of hair.

She immediately lifted her own hand, combed her fingers through her hair and lightly touched the bandage on her forehead.

"Head hurting?" he asked.

"A little. Not bad."

"It's about time for your next pill."

"Are you trying to keep me drugged?"

"Guilty as charged. How else am I going to get you to take it easy?"

Her smile was so natural, so soft and welcoming, that his stomach gave a jolt. His hands fairly itched to draw her to him, to hold that compact body against his, forget about the rest of the world—intruders, jobs in another city, daily life.

"I see you sold the lace-patterned, rococo pitcher." She walked over to the shelf to rearrange the tall cup and lace-edged saucer on the tray. "Who bought it?"

"Norah Conway."

"Ah. She's a good customer. Deep pockets, too. You couldn't talk her into the whole set?"

He hadn't even thought of it. He'd been in the process of shifting all the china stuff to one place, and the woman had walked in and seen him with the pitcher in his hand. She'd snatched it up and bought it on the spot.

"I don't think she saw the rest of the set."

"What do you mean? The pitcher was sitting right here on the tray." At that moment, she seemed to come awake like a startled bird. Her green eyes snapped wide and she took a good look around the room.

Colby waited for her words of praise at how he'd changed things.

"Oh, my gosh. It *wasn't* sitting on the tray. What in the world have you done to my store?"

"Like it?"

"Like...? Darn it, Colby, you've got all the china shoved together. And...and my candles! Criminy. Did you use a ruler to get them that straight?"

His back teeth ground together. Becca Sue could get his goat quicker than anyone he knew. "Of course I didn't use a ruler. But you have to agree this is a much better setup. I mean, how can your customers find anything if you have it strewn all over the store without a single theme?"

"That's the point. You draw them down the aisles

where they can be delighted with each new treasure they come upon. If someone comes in looking for a book, they're not going to browse the china aisle, they'll go where the books are. If there's a tea set among the volumes of poetry, then perhaps they'll remember a gift they intended to buy for a family member—or even for themselves. It's called creative marketing. And I'm very good at it."

He folded his arms across his chest. That sort of reasoning didn't make sense to his orderly mind. Granted, this wasn't his shop, but he'd made a personal commitment to be here for the next little while.

Clearly, one of them was going to have to learn to bend a bit more. And in his opinion, that someone ought to be Becca.

Chapter Seven

The next morning, Becca looked out the front store window and saw Tracy Lynn's car parked at the curb. Since her friend wasn't in her shop, she figured it was hair day, and she'd be at Donetta's.

And that's exactly what Becca needed. A hair day.

She actually shuddered at the thought of leaving Colby alone in her shop, but she only intended to be gone long enough for a shampoo and blow dry. How much damage could he do in that amount of time?

Plenty, an inner demon taunted.

She hadn't had the energy to reposition her merchandise. He'd reorganized her coffee and flavored syrups, as well as her shop items, but she could live with that change. That was housekeeping, not merchandising.

Darn it, he was trying. Skeeter had stopped by yesterday as promised and taken a more detailed report, then helped Colby install new locks on both the front and back doors.

Now she had dead bolts guarding her store, and Colby Flynn guarding her person.

Lord have mercy!

Sighing, she walked the two doors down to Donetta's Secret and pushed through the door. The salon was decorated in a trendy style to match its owner's personality—leopard-print carpet, lipstick-red walls, sparkling mirrors and gleaming Sputnik light fixtures. It wasn't a large salon, just four work-stations, the same number of hair-dryer chairs and two shampoo bowls. Donetta usually worked two chairs at a time, and the other two were invariably occupied by friends just visiting, as Tracy Lynn was now.

Tracy jumped up the minute Becca pushed through the door.

"Becca! What are you doing walking around? Sit, for heaven's sake."

"Don't you dare coddle me. I've had it up to here with that." She made a slicing motion at her throat with her good hand.

"You're such a brat," Tracy Lynn said lovingly. "You never want to accept anyone's help."

"Well, I'm about to ruin your opinion of me because that's exactly what I need. I feel so darn helpless and ridiculous. I can manage to take a bath, but I can't wash my hair."

Donetta laughed. "Well, then, you've come to the right place."

"Absolutely," Tracy Lynn said. "In fact, I'll wash it for you while Netta finishes up with Anna."

Anna—Donetta's mother-in-law—reached out a

hand for Becca's. "I can't believe you had a break-in. You poor love. Is there anything I can do?"

"Anna, you've done plenty by stocking my refrigerator with delicious meals." Anna's Café had been the hangout spot for Becca, Sunny, Donetta and Tracy Lynn most of their lives. Of course, until just a year ago, it had been named Wanda's. But Anna had bought it and though the decor had changed—for the better—it was still the hub of the town.

That was one of the things Becca loved so much about Hope Valley. Between Anna's Café, Donetta's Secret and Becca's Attic, Main Street was *the* gathering spot. One could invariably find a friend or loved one just by driving down the street and glancing through the storefront windows. Theirs was a close-knit community that was more like a family.

And that thought made her wonder again who would have broken into her shop. And *attacked* her.

"Thank you for the sandwiches and casserole you brought by yesterday," Becca said to Anna. "I'd have called, but I was a little out of it. The day was a blur."

"You're very welcome, hon. I'm just so upset that this happened to you. We simply don't have this sort of thing going on in Hope Valley. You can be sure I'll be keeping a close eye on any out-of-town customers. And eavesdropping, as well. We need to get to the bottom of this."

"Thanks, Anna. Hopefully Storm's fingerprint computers will turn up something. Meanwhile, Colby's determined to play bodyguard. He thinks he scared the intruder off, and evidently the heroic deed has gone to his head. He's doing everything short of flexing his muscles."

The girls and Anna laughed. "I must say, I was pleased to see that Colby had things well under control when I stopped by."

"Ha. That's a matter of opinion." Becca squeezed Anna's hand, then followed Tracy Lynn over to the shampoo bowl and sat. "Where are the babies?"

"In the back sleeping," Tracy said.

Becca should have figured as much. Donetta tried to keep the babies away from the chemical smells of hair dye and perm solution as much as possible. She'd even put a portable air purifier unit in the back room to insure that Amanda's and Chelsa's little lungs didn't absorb anything harsh.

Becca thought it was neat that her friends' children would all grow up so close in age. Would they form a bond as their mothers had? Become the Texas Sweethearts II? Donetta's daughter was only four months older than Tracy Lynn's baby. Although Tracy Lynn had miscarried with her first pregnancy, she and her husband, Linc, hadn't wasted any time and she'd soon been pregnant again. Then Sunny and Jack had announced their good news. At one point, three of the Texas Sweethearts had been pregnant at the same time—albeit, Sunny in the very early stages.

Becca had been the only one of the group not experiencing morning sickness, stretch marks, swollen ankles, maternity clothes…and the sheer glow of happiness at the miracle of a baby growing in her womb.

Stifling her envy had been no easy feat. But she'd managed.

Just then, Sunny Slade, looking as though she were ready to have her baby any minute now, walked in with her seven-year-old daughter, Tori.

"Grandma!" Tori called, skipping over to Anna.

Sunny headed straight for Becca as Tracy Lynn helped her lean her head back against the shiny black shampoo bowl.

Donetta grinned. "Hmm, this ought to be interesting. The last time Tracy Lynn and Sunny were next to the same shampoo bowl, there was a water fight."

Tracy Lynn sniffed. "I'm sure we've matured since then. We are, after all, mothers."

"I was a mother then," Sunny pointed out—although not officially at the time. Tori was Jackson Slade's daughter from a previous marriage, and Sunny had adopted her after she and Jack had married. "However, I know enough not to chance getting Becca's bandage and stitches wet. How are you?" she asked, her distended stomach nearly brushing Becca's face.

"Fine except for the humiliation of having to ask for help to bathe, dress and wash my hair."

"Bathing and dressing?" Sunny asked. Both she and Tracy Lynn looked at each other, then over at Donetta, who had an application squeeze bottle suspended in midair. Anna, wiping her forehead with a towel so the hair dye wouldn't drip into her eyes, had turned in the chair. Cora Harriet——Sunny and Jack's housekeeper, who was sitting under the hair dryer—raised the heat hood and cocked an ear.

Criminy, Becca thought. She should have known better than to open her mouth without guarding her words. After all, the whole darn town knew that Colby Flynn was staying with her.

"It's all perfectly platonic," she said. *Not.* "So, get your minds out of the gutter."

"My mind wasn't anywhere near the gutter," Tracy Lynn drawled, testing the temperature of the water and applying the spray hose to Becca's hair. "Was y'alls?" she asked Sunny and the room at large.

Donetta, Anna and Cora uttered a chorus of "nos."

Sunny fluffed her naturally curly, blond hair. "Actually, mine was. I want to hear about the bathing and dressing."

Becca turned her head to glare at her friend and got an earful of water.

"Would you be still!" Tracy demanded. "I'm trying not to get these stitches wet. Lordy!" She glanced at Sunny. "Baby hormones?" she asked compassionately.

"Yes. I feel like a huge cow and can't imagine anything remotely sexy about getting help with my toiletries. So I'm trying to live vicariously through my friends."

"Oh, for goodness sake, Sunny," Becca said.

"Your husband is totally sappy when it comes to your Madonna-like form. He thinks you're the sexiest thing on the planet!" Good thing Tori was in the back hovering over the babies.

"All right, girls," Anna said, clearing her throat. "Too much information."

They all looked at Anna and laughed. She might be Sunny's mother, but she'd been the confidante of all four of the Texas Sweethearts at one time or another.

Sunny grabbed a towel and helpfully shielded Becca's forehead and stitches from the water. The tail of the towel draped over Becca's eyes so she couldn't see the expression on anyone's face. Just as well.

"So," Tracy Lynn said, "want to fill us in on your nursemaid and his helpfulness?"

"I can hold my hands over Anna's ears," Donetta volunteered.

"Don't you dare," Anna said. "I don't mind hearing the down and dirty of what goes on in Becca Sue's household. It's just my daughter that I'm a little skittish about. Besides, Cora's not going to put that hair dryer back over her head until she's sure she won't miss anything, and I'm not going to be left out of the loop."

Becca sighed and melted into the bowl as Tracy Lynn massaged shampoo into her hair and scalp. She hadn't realized how tense she'd been these past couple of days.

"There's nothing to miss," she said. "Colby's got

his office phone forwarding calls to his cell and he's doing business from my shop while he helps out with the customers. And yes, he's had to assist in putting plastic over this brace, but I assure you I'm perfectly capable of bathing on my own. Happy now?" she asked, moving the towel out of her face so she could strain her gaze around the room.

"We were happy before," Donetta commented easily. "It's just that we're *happier* when someone's sharing. Right, girls?"

"Right," everyone in the room chorused—except Becca, of course.

Tracy Lynn finger-combed conditioner through the strands of wet hair, then rinsed it out. The tropical scent of the products wafting up from the bowl nearly transported Becca to a dreamy Hawaiian island.

When Tracy shut off the water, Sunny blotted moisture from Becca's forehead, careful of the stitches, and wrapped the terry cloth towel around her head, helping her sit up.

"Thanks, you two. That felt wonderful."

"Anytime. What are friends for if not to wash your hair for you?"

For some stupid reason, a lump of emotion rose in Becca's throat. She was blessed with such good friends. She couldn't imagine being without them, or living anywhere else except for right here in Hope Valley. These people were her family, wonderful replacements for her real family, who were all gone.

"Colby's got a job offer in Dallas," she blurted. "He's supposed to leave in three weeks."

Tracy Lynn and Sunny stared, wide-eyed. Donetta and Anna looked sad. Cora had lowered her hair dryer hood, but now had it up again.

"I ran into Darla Pam over at Hansen's the other day," Becca went on, "and she was spouting off some gossip about Colby leaving. I thought she was just trying to get a rise out of me, and I tuned her out. I mean, Colby and I haven't been close in a long time, but why would he keep something like that from me? Why would he let it become the center of the gossip mill before I'd heard it? That's what I was thinking. Guess I placed a little more importance on my role in his life—or past role—than was actually there. Now, aren't you all feeling silly that you were trying to read so much importance into his helping me out?"

"I don't feel a damn bit silly," Donetta said. "I saw how he looked at you the other night. He was scared to death and worried out of his mind. I'd say you *still* play a big role in his life."

Becca shook her head. "He's accepted a partnership at a firm in Dallas. And I'm happy for him. It's no big deal. What we had was over seven years ago."

"You sure about that?" Tracy Lynn asked.

"Of course I'm sure. We can hardly be civil for more than a day. My God, did you know that he threw out Maizy?"

"No!" Anna exclaimed. "Surely not."

"Why would he do something like that?" Tracy Lynn's look of horror matched everyone else's.

Becca didn't even give it a second thought that

these women knew she'd named her sourdough starter. There was very little they all didn't know about one another. Anna and Cora included, as both women had had a hand in raising the four of them.

"He claimed he was cleaning out my fridge. Did I *ask* him to clean out my fridge? No," she answered before anyone else could. "I didn't. Nor did I ask him to put away my appliances or hide my dish soap. I mean, I *work* in my kitchen, for pity's sake. I cook and bake and…and I *like* to have my appliances and dish soap and sponges at my fingertips. Mr. Neatnik breaks out in hives unless every surface is uncluttered, grouped according to texture, size, color and usability, *and* has a mirror shine to it."

A thoughtful, knowing hum buzzed through the salon as Becca stood and made her way over to Donetta's chair, which Anna had vacated.

"So what's going on with your hand?" Donetta asked, obviously feeling a subject change was in order before Becca blew a gasket.

"I'm supposed to go back Friday and have another X-ray."

"Why wait so long if it's broken? Shouldn't they be putting a cast on it?"

"The doctors probably don't want to do a cast until the swelling goes down and they can get a better look at the injury," Sunny said. "Could be the fracture's so minor it'll heal without the aid of a cast. It might just be a really bad bruise, which can often be more painful than an actual break. Either way, Becca's not going to be kneading bread dough or opening jars or dealing with small buttons any time soon."

Hearing Sunny restate what the emergency doctor had said was actually comforting. After all, bones were bones, be they animal or human, and Sunny had dealt with plenty of fractures and bruises in her veterinary practice.

As she was thinking about veterinarians, another thought struck. She glanced at Sunny.

"Colby told me that Bosco died last week."

Sunny gasped. "Oh, no. He was such a sweetheart of a dog. I knew it was coming, but I didn't think it'd be this soon."

"Evidently it was peaceful. He took Bosco with him to Houston, and he died in his sleep."

"He must be devastated."

"I think so. You know Colby. He'll sweet-talk you and make you think he doesn't have a care in the world, but he feels things deeply."

"Think he'll get another dog?" Sunny asked.

"He didn't mention anything about it. Besides, he's moving. I imagine he'll wait until he's settled. You never know, he might end up living in a condo in the city or someplace that wouldn't be suitable for a dog."

"Little dogs can live anywhere," Donetta said. Storm had a little dog, a terrier named Sneaker, and though he and Donetta lived on several acres, Sneaker would probably have been happy with just a patio.

"Do you mean to say he's moving before he makes living arrangements?" Tracy asked.

Becca shrugged and her head bobbed back as Donetta worked a brush through the short strands. "I didn't ask. I was just so stunned that he was moving at all."

"Has anyone talked to Katherine Durant?" Anna asked. "She'd know if he's listed his house."

Becca felt her stomach tumble. She loved that old farmhouse Colby lived in. It had originally been the McGivers's place, and Becca and her friends had gone there many a Sunday afternoon when they were children, or sometimes spent the weekend and rode to church with the McGivers. Arlene McGiver had been their Sunday school teacher. She and her husband didn't have children of their own, and they delighted in entertaining other people's kids.

Becca remembered times in the huge country kitchen, baking banana bread and scones. It had been Arlene who'd given the sourdough mash recipe to Becca's mother and grandmother.

All three women were gone—Mama, Grandma Lee and Arlene McGiver.

And now the bread starter was, too.

Lord, she didn't like the direction of her thoughts, the loneliness they conjured up. Soon, Colby would be gone. Not dead like the rest of her family, thank God, but away, nonetheless. To a life in another town clear across the state. She wouldn't wake up in the mornings and see him opening the door of his law office, wouldn't run into him in the post office or at the counter in Anna's Café.

He wouldn't be right across the street to save her

from intruders wielding big sticks and with criminal intentions.

He wouldn't be around to make good on that crazy baby pact.

She knew it was foolish to give any thought to those drunken words spoken all those years ago on the eve of their breakup. Nobody made promises like that. It was stupid to even imagine such a thing.

But stupid or not, Becca *did* imagine it. All too vividly.

THE TRIP TO THE BEAUTY SALON was more tiring than Becca had anticipated, and afterward, she'd gone straight up to her apartment for a nap, then had a light supper and gone back to bed. When she awoke again, it was after 9:00 p.m. and her arm and head were begging for pain meds.

Was all this sleeping a delayed reaction to the break-in and assault two days ago? And had she simply become so comfortable with Colby's presence, trusting him to watch over what was hers, that she could indulge in all the sleep she needed?

Maybe she had.

She got out of bed, splashed water on her face one-handed, then made her way out to the kitchen. Colby stood with his back to her, squinting at a computer printout of some sort. In front of him, lined along the countertop, were the flour canister, the sugar container, a package of yeast and a mixing bowl. As one might see on those fancy cooking shows or infomercials, he had small bowls lined up in front of each ingredient container, obviously so he could measure out everything in advance and have it ready to pour into the main mixing bowl. A lot of wasted steps if you asked her—and extra dishes to wash.

But then, Colby had his way of doing things, and she had hers. Usually, they'd both end up with the same—or nearly the same—results.

"What's up?" she asked, causing him to jump. Now that was interesting. He wasn't a man easily spooked.

"You're supposed to be resting."

The faint trace of accusation and annoyance in his tone didn't trigger her usual ire. In fact, she nearly smiled.

"Couldn't sleep. I came in to try some warm milk or a pain pill."

He frowned and glanced at his watch. "I gave you a pain pill two hours ago."

"I didn't take it."

"Why the hell not?"

"Because it makes me have nightmares. Besides, I thought I could get by with some Tylenol or Motrin." She nodded to his assembly on the countertop. "What are you making?"

"Matilda."

"Excuse me?"

"I killed Maizy, so I'm attempting to resurrect her through Matilda. She might not be as long in the tooth as Maizy or have been handed down through all those generations, but if the lady on the Internet site is honest, then Matilda ought to be able to step into Maizy's shoes—or at least her stinky jar."

Becca nearly laughed at him talking about a concoction of flour, water, sugar and yeast as if it were a living, breathing person.

But the fact was, she was incredibly touched.

He wasn't making fun of her naming her bread dough. He was giving her, and her baking, the respect he obviously felt it deserved.

And apologizing, as well. Very nicely. An "I'm sorry" would have been okay. Instead, he was *showing* her his apology.

Why, oh why, did what she want out of life have to scare him so?

She pulled up a chair. "Want some help?"

"No. I need to figure this out on my own. I found out it's not so strange that you named the other goop. Did you know there's a recipe on the Internet named Herman?"

She started to nod.

"Then there's the kind you make with potato water. You don't suppose that's what the Sunday school teacher used, do you?"

"I'm pretty sure she just used plain old lukewarm water."

"Lukewarm?" he asked.

"To dissolve the yeast." He was so cute, staring at his ingredients and recipe as though this were a scientific experiment of epic proportions.

"Okay. I think I'm headed in the right direction, then. According to this paper, it doesn't look like I can screw up too badly." He grinned at her. "I might not be your Grandma Lee, but at least when I leave, Matilda will have a memory attached to her. She'll be a little part of me."

He said it teasingly, but Becca's heart saw a completely different meaning to the words.

A little part of me.

A baby.

Lordy, she was like a broken record. She needed to toss that maudlin sucker out and get on with life, or at least think in modern term clichés like compact disks rather than records.

And that dumb thought made her seriously doubt her sanity, so when Colby wiped his hands on a dish towel, shook out a pain pill from the bottle and held it out to her, she was reluctant to take it. Something was surely causing a short circuit in her brain, and she needed all her wits about her to fix the problem.

"Come on, sugar pie. Now that you've admitted you're not taking the pills I give you, I'm gonna stand over you and watch you closer."

"You can certainly try." Although it wasn't her intention, she said the words as a challenge. Still, she took the pill and glass of water from him, and swallowed.

"Did you hear anything from Storm on the fingerprints?" she asked.

"Nothing's turned up in the database—except for Miz Lloyd's prints, but I doubt she was the one who clobbered you."

She saw the teasing light in his eyes, as well as the worry that they didn't know any more about the intruder than they had Sunday night.

"Does Millie have a record for something?"

"I asked Storm the same thing," he said, lining up his ingredient bowls with more military precision. "I guess years ago she applied for a daycare-center license. In order to obtain one, you have to have your prints on file with the state."

"I never knew she ran a daycare center. That must have been quite a while ago." But Becca *did* know that Millicent and Harold had wanted children of their own and had never been blessed with them.

Something Becca and Millie shared.

She set aside that thought. "So how'd you manage to get a partnership in a Dallas law firm?" she asked, determined to confront the issue of him leaving and be done with it. Perhaps then her imagination would stop leaping on his bones. "Is either Wells or Steadman a close friend or something?"

"Wells's daughter. Cassandra." He squinted at the recipe in front of him, then held up the four-cup glass measure, giving it a little shake to settle the flour.

Becca didn't bother to tell him that if the recipe had called for *sifted* flour, he'd just messed up his measurements. First off, she didn't think it was that vital to the total outcome of the starter, and secondly, he was anal enough without her adding to it.

"We've dated off and on for a few years," he continued, his words effectively jerking Becca to attention. "She recommended me to her father. It grew from there."

"Oh." Becca's stomach hit bottom. She hadn't realized he was dating anyone. "Does Cassandra work at the firm as well?"

"Not yet, but soon. She was a stockbroker until her dad convinced her to go to law school and follow in his footsteps. She still needs to pass the bar exam. She'll make it, though. She's sharp."

His tone held a great deal of respect and affection. Becca didn't think he'd lived like a monk all these years—shoot, she'd dated other men over the past seven years. Still, to have it come straight from the horse's mouth…well, it was a bit of a shock.

And a huge wake-up call.

Lord, she was a fool.

Here she'd been making herself a wreck, thinking he could possibly have unresolved feelings for *her,* and all along the man had a *girlfriend!*

A girlfriend who was fixing to be an attorney.

How could Becca compete with that? Her world was here in a small town selling antiques and trinkets, and knitting baby blankets and booties. Not exactly high society.

Colby had always wanted more. More money. More prestige.

He walked a different social path than she did.

She'd never been the type to think that someone else was better than her, nor had she ever been lacking in self-confidence. But hearing him describe Cassandra, Becca felt out of her league.

She should have known, should have remembered. She still believed that one of the reasons they weren't together as a couple was that he hadn't found her goals sophisticated enough, hadn't loved her enough to continue their relationship—or to convince her to give *his* world a try

He'd made it clear seven years ago that he didn't want white picket fences and barefoot babies, nor did he want sweet little Becca Sue Ellsworth from Hope Valley, Texas.

His style and tastes had changed.

Obviously to sharp-as-a-tack, soon-to-be-attorney Cassandra Wells.

Chapter Eight

"How come you're not wearing your sling?" Colby asked the next day as he knelt next to the shelves and unpacked a shipment of yarn. Many more of these kinds of deliveries and she'd have to rename the place Becca's yarns.

"It rubs on my neck."

He set aside the purchase order receipt and stood, spying the blue sling lying on the front counter by the register. He picked it up and approached Becca.

"Colby—"

"No arguments, sugar pie. Tomorrow we go see the doc." He was surprised how fast the week was passing. There had been no more break-in attempts and they still didn't have any suspects. He was relieved about the first thing, and edgy about the latter. He wouldn't be here to watch over Becca Sue forever.

But he was here now and determined to do his part.

"Until you get the official okay, you need to keep

this thing on." He looped the sling over her head, eased her arm into the cradle of fabric, then ran his fingers around the part where she complained it was chafing her neck.

She shivered and their gazes locked. Man alive, his control was only hanging on by a thread these days. He needed a distraction.

"Hey, I've got a cool idea," he said, noticing the white yarn peeking out of her knitting bag. He snatched it up, figuring they could use it as a cushion between her neck and the scratchy sling fabric.

"No! Wait!"

Her near scream scared the devil out of him and he jumped back. He heard metal hit the floor. "What is wrong with you?"

"What is wrong with *you?*" she countered, cupping her uninjured hand beneath his, cradling the yarn as though they were holding a fragile baby. "Didn't you notice that's a sweater in progress? Tracy Lynn picked the pattern and asked me to knit it. My gosh, that's cashmere yarn and it cost the earth."

He gingerly held the tightly knitted, baby-soft yarn. A bunch of empty little loops stared up at him. Even *he* knew that cashmere was expensive. "Sorry. Now what?"

"Now we need to thread the needle back through the stitches without dropping any."

He didn't know why she said *we*. *He* certainly didn't knit. As for Becca Sue fixing his screwup, he could see right away this was going to be a problem since she had the full use of only one hand. "Don't some of your girlfriends knit?"

"Some of them."

"Then why don't we, real ginger-like, put this away and one of the girls can help you out later?"

She studied him for a long moment. "Mama used to say if you make a mess, don't expect someone else to clean it up."

"And you took that advice to heart, didn't you," he said with amused sarcasm, meaning her habit of leaving clothes and clutter lying all around.

He noted the devilish spark in her eyes, and realized they weren't on the same page at all. Becca was totally unrepentant about leaving her clothes right where she stepped out of them, or letting a stack of books overflow onto the floor. She didn't consider those messes, she'd told him, because she lived alone and knew that she was the only one who would pick them up and that eventually she'd get around to it.

This mess she was talking about now was right here in his hands.

"Oh, no," he said. "I don't know anything about yarn and knitting, and I don't want to, either."

"'Fraid somebody will see you and question your masculinity?"

A challenge. He gritted his teeth. The little minx knew he couldn't resist a taunt like that. "No, I'm not *afraid*."

"Well, then?"

"Fine. I'll see what I can do." Pulling his cupped

hands away from her, he sank into the overstuffed chair she'd vacated, rested his elbows on his knees and carefully let the knitting drape over his hands. Becca Sue held the end of the yarn, keeping a good amount of slack in it, obviously so the whole shebang wouldn't start to unravel.

She perched on the rolled arm of the chair, bent her head right next to his, their cheeks nearly touching. He could feel her warm breath on his skin, practically taste the peach preserves and coffee she'd had with breakfast this morning.

Slowly, he turned his head, gazed in her eyes, saw her lick her lips. He could kiss her right now. It would be so easy. Just lean forward a fraction of an inch and he'd be able to feel the softness of that sexy bottom lip, explore the mouth he hadn't sampled in seven long years.

"What?" she whispered.

He leaned back and cleared his throat. What the hell was he thinking? "You're in my light."

"Oh." She hopped up and dragged a floor lamp over to the chair.

"Damn it, Becca. I could have done that. You've got no business hauling the furniture around in your condition."

"My condition? You make it sound like I'm pregnant." The minute the P-word slipped out of her mouth, she froze.

Colby's eyes locked onto hers.

"Um…forget I just said that," she stammered.

He shook his head, exhaled a weary sigh.

"That's like telling me to ignore an elephant in the middle of the room."

No truer words had ever been spoken, Becca thought. But right now she'd much rather be discussing pachyderms than pregnancy.

She cleared her throat and brought her mind back to knitting. "Now, you need to hold the needle in your left hand—"

"I'm right-handed."

"That's fine. I'm left-handed, but I knit right-handed—"

"A switch hitter, hum?"

"I suppose. Grandma Lee was right-handed, and she taught me to knit her way." She pointed to the yarn in his hands. "You pulled the stitches off the left needle, so you've got to thread it back through so that this tail of yarn I'm holding ends up at the top."

"Great. I have a feeling this is going to be about as easy as teaching a mermaid to do the splits."

She chuckled. "Just take it slow. Slide it in nice and gentle...that's the way," she coached as he threaded the needle through a loop.

He shifted in the chair, tried to put a little more space between them. By God, he was beginning to sweat.

"I think I can handle it without the commentary." He hooked the next loop.

"No, clearly you can't. You just entered that one—"

"Damn it!" he exclaimed. "Are these really knitting terms? 'Take it slow,'" he mimicked. "'Slide it in nice and gentle.'"

He saw Becca's cheeks flame. Good. He didn't want to be the only one squirming in his chair.

"Actually, I was trying *not* to talk in knitting terms so you'd understand better."

"Yeah, well, I'm smarter than I look, so give me a quick seminar in the terminology. You don't have enough of this sweater knitted to use as a cover in case a customer comes in."

Her gaze dipped to his crotch.

"Yes, I'm aroused," he said. "You're sexy as all get out, you smell good enough to eat and I damned well wasn't the only one who was thinking about kissing a couple of minutes ago. Then next thing I know, you're purring in my ear as though we're having phone sex."

She jumped up off the edge of the chair and paced around the counter. He saw her chest rise as she drew in a deep breath.

Hell, this little episode wasn't even half of the problem. Every morning, he walked out of her bedroom stiff as a board. Did she think it was *easy* to hook her bra, then pretend his thoughts were as innocent as a Boy Scout's?

After a couple of minutes, she came back around the counter and sat down again on the edge of the chair.

"Okay. There are two types of knitting stitches. A knit stitch and a purl stitch. I've used both in this piece. The purl stitch has a little nub—"

"Becca," he warned between clenched teeth. God almighty, he couldn't get his mind off sex.

She whacked him on the shoulder.

"Hey. What was that for?"

"To jolt your brain out of its one-track groove."

"I saw you over there gathering your composure. You're just as turned-on as I am."

"Maybe so. But I'm not going to do anything about it—except make sure you get my stitches back on that knitting needle correctly. Now, the purl stitch has a round knot facing you. Think of it as a noose around somebody's neck—*yours,* with me doing the tightening if you mess this up. The knit stitch looks like a flat V—picture a scarf folded one side over the other."

"Right over left, or left over right?"

"I don't know! Either way. It looks like a flat V. Do you see either of those images?"

He looked close. "Yeah. I see it. The purl looks more like a knot on a man's tie than a hangman's noose."

"Clearly, you're a calmer knitter than I am. Now, you need to make sure you get all these stitches back on the needle going the same direction." She guided his hand with hers, showing him what she meant.

It was slow going, and using his left hand was about as awkward as holding a handful of frogs, but he was getting the hang of it. "Thank God Tracy Lynn's small," he muttered. "If this was a blanket, it'd take all week—"

"Oops," she mumbled when he hooked a stitch back to front.

He whipped his head around and glared at her. "I see it." He backed the knitting needle out and hooked the stitch the correct way.

He was two stitches from the end when Lincoln Slade poked his head in the door.

"I'm trying to track down my wife and baby girl," he said. "You seen two beautiful blondes come by this way?"

Colby snapped his knees closed and kept his hands between them, hoping to hide the yarn. He saw Becca smile sweetly at Linc. The man was a tough-guy horse breeder and all-around softie when it came to his socialite wife and tiny baby.

"It's Wednesday," Becca said. "She's usually over at the seniors center painting fingernails or something."

"Yeah, I know, but she said she might stop by here first and see if you needed help."

"She did, but Colby sent her on her way."

Linc grinned at Colby. "You plannin' on joinin' the stitch-and-gripe group, pal?"

Colby shot Linc a look that had the other man laughing and holding up his hands in surrender. "Right. Catch you two later." Linc backed out the door, still chuckling.

"I don't know why you had to look at him in that tone of voice," Becca said. "Men knit and crochet just like women do."

Colby hooked the last two stitches, then shoved the whole mess way down on the needles so they wouldn't slide off again. Then he folded the knitted yarn around the needles for added protection and placed it in her knitting bag.

"Back to square one on padding the sling," he said, looking around the shop and ignoring her comment about men knitting. Truthfully, it probably wouldn't be such a bad hobby if the whole stereotypical thing wasn't involved. He could see how the rhythm of moving stitches from one needle to the next might be a good exercise for stress relief. Unless, of course, some yahoo dumped the needle out of the loops.

In any case, he'd just as soon work out his stress on a basketball court or with a three-mile run.

Before he could locate a suitable cushion for Becca's sling, he spied Trouble on the floor, batting around something shiny. He retrieved the silver clip and looked around the shop for a jar or bin that she might keep such an item in. He didn't see anything that gave him a clue, but then again, what did he expect? Becca had a weird shelving system.

"Where's this go?" he asked, holding up the clip. He saw that she was fixing to pour a cup of coffee, and he moved over next to her, took the carafe out of her hand and did it for her, stirring in a splash of cream.

"I'm not helpless, but thank you. Where does what go?"

"This clip. Trouble was playing with it on the floor."

Becca sighed and gave the cat a stern look. "Oh, Trouble. Why can't you bring me mice like a normal cat?"

Colby raised an eyebrow, waiting for her to elaborate.

"My cat is a thief. He steals from the neighbors. That clip obviously came from Donetta's salon." She took the clip and put it in a bowl by the cash register. "It's embarrassing to have to go around returning things this little menace has stolen. Once he brought me a fifty-dollar bill. Snatched it right out of Darla Pam Kirkwell's purse."

"How'd you know it was Darla Pam's?"

"I just listened for who was yelling the loudest. I guess she went to pay Donetta for her hairdo and came up short of money. I was pacing the sidewalk, trying to find a tactful way of asking the neighbors if they were missing fifty bucks, and heard the commotion. To this day, I don't think Darla Pam believes me that Trouble took the money."

She retrieved a piece of thin foam rubber from behind the counter and passed it to him, along with a pair of scissors. "I use this when I'm shipping fragile merchandise. You can cut a piece and see if it'll cushion the sling at my neck."

"Guess I should have thought of this in the first place before I nearly ruined Tracy Lynn's sweater."

"Oh, you didn't come close to ruining it. I'd have fixed it when my hand got better. I can't do anything with it until the splint comes off, anyway."

He put his hands on his hips, scissors in one hand, the foam in the other. "If it was no big deal, how come you squawked like I'd plucked your prize rooster?"

She laughed at him. "That was a perfectly natural reaction. I thought about the dollar signs first and logic second." She shrugged. "Besides, I wanted to see if you could—or *would*—try to make it right."

"Well, did I pass the test?"

"With flying colors. You know, knitting circles can be a lot of fun. Think of all the gossip you'd get to hear."

"Don't even go there, sugar pie. As it is, I'll probably have to chew some nails or eat a lightbulb next time I see Linc—just so he won't be looking at me funny."

"Colby Flynn, even a fool wouldn't question your masculinity. Knitting needles or not."

"Mmm. Compliments from Becca Sue. I like that." He puffed out his chest. "I'm feeling better already."

"Yes, well, my neck isn't. So if you want me to keep this darn sling on, you'd better get over here with that foam."

"Yes, ma'am. Right away." Any excuse to touch Becca Sue's soft skin. He didn't have to be asked twice.

THEY HAD A STEADY STREAM of customers most of the day, and Becca was feeling a little wilted. Colby noticed.

He moved up next to her, bent his knees and looked her in the eye. "Ready to call it a day?"

"Yes. I think I am."

"Man, you must be feeling poorly. I never thought you'd agree to closing the shop early."

"Twenty minutes isn't much."

He gently pressed his lips to the bandage over her forehead, startling her.

"Colby…?

"A kiss to make it better." He turned and headed for the front door, evidently to lock it and flip over the Closed sign.

She swallowed hard. Why did he have to do things like that? Sure, under other circumstances, that gentle press of lips could be considered just a friendly sort of gesture. But living with Colby 24/7 was making it very clear that she had more than *friendly* feelings for him.

And when he did things like this, it just messed with her emotions all the more. But if she made a big deal out of it, she'd give herself away.

Criminy, this trying-to-be-sophisticated stuff was difficult.

Ever since Colby had told her about Cassandra, Becca had been acutely aware of her own behavior, and tried to make sure that she acted and reacted in a manner that would be considered sophisticated. She didn't always succeed. Most of the time, she totally forgot and just acted like herself.

Which wasn't a bad thing. She owned her own business, for crying out loud. No country bumpkin there. Ms. Not-yet-an-attorney Cassandra Wells couldn't claim the right of being her own boss. So, neener, neener.

Becca gave a mental groan. Now *that* had been a real mature, sophisticated thought!

Darn it. Why in the world was she questioning herself? If the man would just keep his lips and his sexy hands and voice to himself, they'd get along fine. Her hand would heal and he could be on his way. But no, he had to comment on the way she smelled, or compliment the way she looked, or let his hands linger just a tad longer than necessary when he was hooking her bra.

By dog, she was going to stop wearing the thing, see-through top or not. She'd put on a sweater and turn up the air-conditioning.

Caught up in her thoughts, it was a moment before she became aware of Sunny's voice from the front door. Becca sighed. Looked like they wouldn't be closing early, after all.

"Girl, you are really waddling these days," Becca teased her friend. She noticed that Colby had taken the purselike carrier out of Sunny's hands. A gentlemanly thing to do. With her stomach stretching the seams of her maternity top, it appeared that even carrying a small purse was too great of a burden.

"Thank you so much for pointing that out, Becca Sue. Just you wait. One of these days you'll be in this position and I'll be happy to pick on you."

Her heart felt another momentary sting. She'd give just about anything to be in Sunny's condition.

"So what's in the carrier?" she asked, masking her emotions.

A high-pitched bark sounded in answer. Colby set the carrier down on the countertop. Sunny unzipped the mesh flap, reached inside and drew out the most pitiful-looking dog Becca had ever seen. The hair on its body was totally shaved, except for a little white tuft on its tail and some wisps of white on its feet. The hair on its face was short, white around the nose, black on the ears, and black around the eyes like a bandit. Sticking straight up along the center of its head was a white stripe of hair like a skunk's.

"Meet Tinky-Winky," Sunny said, passing the little dog to Colby's arms.

Colby looked utterly confused and unsure as he accepted the dog. Well, he couldn't have done anything else. Sunny didn't give him a choice.

"Tinky-Winky?" His tone bordered on disgust. "What kind of name is that for a dog?"

Sunny shrugged. "It was on his collar. Somebody abandoned him out on the highway by our ranch. His hair was matted beyond grooming, so I had to shave him. Plus, he has a skin allergy. I've been treating him for that, plus malnutrition and dehydration."

"What breed of dog is he?" Becca asked, moving next to Colby so she could stroke the little pup. Its shaved body resembled the smooth skin of a baby seal. "Oh, sweetheart, don't shake," she crooned, kissing its floppy ear.

"Hard to say exactly," Sunny said. "There's quite a bit of Yorkie in him—Yorkshire terrier," she clarified, "maybe mixed with Chihuahua and probably some toy poodle."

"How big will he get?"

"Oh, he's full grown. I'd guess he's around two years old." Sunny turned to Colby. "Becca told me that you lost Bosco. I'm so sorry, Colby."

"Thanks."

"Anyway, I've nursed this little guy back to health and it's time he found a home. He needs a place where there aren't big dogs around that'll step on him. I thought maybe since Bosco's gone—"

"Oh, no. Wait a minute. I've got no time for a dog. I'm smack-dab in the middle of moving…hell, I'm not even staying at my own place." The little dog gave a soft whimper and laid its head on Colby's shoulder.

"Aw," Becca and Sunny chorused.

Colby nearly melted. He'd be damned if he would let Becca or Sunny know that, though. The animal's warm body was so small his hand practically wrapped around its belly and back. The thing probably didn't weigh more than five pounds. It was still trembling, and huddling into his neck. He wasn't sure how this creature could even claim to be a dog, it was so pitiful.

"Listen, Colby. You don't have to give me an answer right now. Just keep Tinky for a few days and see how it goes."

"I've got my hands pretty full with Becca."

Becca glared at him. "Surely you're not lumping me in the same category as a dog!"

He backtracked quickly. "Hey, I didn't say anything of the kind."

"He's a good little dog, Colby," Sunny said.

"Once he gets used to you, he'll stop shaking and be more friendly."

"He's pretty friendly already." The mutt still had his head cuddled in the crook of Colby's neck.

"I really can't take him home," Sunny said. "And I can't keep him locked up at the office all the time. It's not fair. No telling what kind of trauma the poor thing went through, or why someone would just dump him on the road like that, but he's well now and he needs to have more freedom—and a loving home. I know he looks kind of sad right now, but I promise he'll be a real cutie when his hair grows back. I've brought kibble, so you won't have to rush right out and buy food. He seems to be fairly well housebroken, and if you get tied up and can't take him outside often enough, he'll use one of these indoor pads if you show him where it is." She held up a square of plastic backed cotton.

"He can stay here," Becca said, completely overriding Colby. She reached for the dog, and he passed it right over. "Oh, you're such a love." She cradled the little dog, shifting it to her shoulder.

Because she was off balance with only one usable hand, Colby put his own hand under Tinky's butt and helped her situate him. Tinky rested his chin on Becca's shoulder, but kept his dark eyes trained on Colby.

Great.

"I think you've found a friend," Becca said to him.

Colby made a noncommittal noise deep in his throat.

"Thanks, guys," Sunny said. "I feel so much better knowing Tinky-Winky won't be locked up in that cage tonight."

When she left, Colby stared at the pitiful excuse for a dog. "The person who saddled this scrawny mutt with that god-awful name ought to be shot."

"It's pretty bad, huh? We can just call him Tinky."

"Poor sucker." He reached out and scratched Tinky's ears. "What do you think, Tink? Want to meet the big bad cat tonight, or wait till you've got the lay of the land better?"

"Oh, I completely forgot about Trouble. We better take this introduction slow. I don't want to traumatize Tinky any more than he's already been."

"Now, don't be making him into a sissy. I imagine he can hold his own." He took the dog from her. "Why don't you head on upstairs and see if the klepto cat's up there before we bring in the dog."

"Okay. Do you think I should put Trouble in the bathroom or something?"

"Probably not. We just want to know where all parties are so there are no surprises. They need to be introduced."

She nodded and headed up the stairs.

When she'd closed the door at the top of the stairwell, Colby set the dog on the floor.

It immediately squatted and peed.

"Hey, now, buddy. What's up with that?" He snatched up some paper towels and pointed his finger at the tiny mutt. "You're two years old, but in dog years, that makes you about sixteen. Teenage boys don't pee on the floor." He stooped down to mop up the mess. Tink sat and watched him.

"Well, at least they don't unless they're drunk or their buddies have egged them on. You're not drunk, and nobody's daring you to pee out here in front of God and everybody. So don't do it again. Got it?"

Tink stood on his hind legs and put his front paws on Colby's knee as if offering an apology.

"Yeah, yeah. I'll let it slide this time, pal. Next time, either use the cat box or ask to go outside."

After locking all the doors to the store, he carried the tiny animal upstairs and locked the stairwell doors behind himself. Living in Hope Valley, Colby had gotten out of the habit of being security-conscious, but he'd made a point of resurrecting the habit since Sunday night's break-in.

When he entered the apartment, Becca was holding the sleek black cat, who took one look at the dog and hissed.

"Now, Trouble. You be nice. Tinky's had a hard life, and you've lived in the lap of luxury all of yours." She looked up at Colby. "What now? Should we set them down?"

"Guess it won't hurt. They'll either go to their corners or come out swinging. Might as well see what we're in for."

Tinky, sensing he'd found a home at last, stopped shaking and instead began to quiver with happiness. Colby knelt and gently put him on the floor, ready to intervene should fur start to fly. Tink plopped down on his butt and stared at Becca. She bent down and let Trouble go.

From there, things got totally out of hand. The cat shot off like a crazed maniac, practically bouncing off the walls and furniture, and the dog scrambled across the floor in a mad chase. Clearly hoping to get away from the creature invading his territory, Trouble leaped through the kitty door, bounded down the stairs and through the cut-out door at the bottom.

Tinky followed, sounding as though he'd rolled down a good many of the steps.

"Oh, no! My antiques!" Becca cried.

"I'll get him." Colby took off after the animals, hollering both their names. Neither one had manners enough to stop or pay him any attention, and before he could get through the doors and get his hands on the quicker-than-lightning, yapping dog, the cat had climbed the drapes and knocked down the shade, a coffee cup Becca had left out had tipped off a spindly legged chair and shattered on the floor and a rack of greeting cards was leaning against the counter like a drunk bellied up to the bar.

Trouble went into hiding, and Tink came to a sliding halt when confronted with a teddy bear that had fallen on the floor.

God help them all. If anyone was still in the saddle shop next door, they'd be calling the sheriff for sure.

Colby frowned as the little dog cowered on its belly and backed away from the stuffed animal.

"Don't tell me you'll chase the cat all over hell and back, but you're scared of a lifeless teddy bear!" He scooped up the dog and plopped it in the armchair. "Stay there so you don't cut your feet." Grabbing the broom, he swept up the broken coffee cup, tossed the debris into the trash can, then picked up the dog.

He stared at the stuffed bear for a minute, then scooped it up, too. Tink trembled and tried to climb right up Colby's neck.

"Settle down, buddy." He went back up the stairs, closed and locked the doors, tossed the teddy bear on the floor in front of the kitty door, then plunked Tink on the couch.

"Is everything okay down there?" Becca asked.

"Pretty much."

"It sounded like a war zone."

"Let's just say the next few days ought to be interesting."

"Why'd you bring the teddy bear up here?"

"The dog seems to be afraid of it. I'm hoping it'll keep him from crossing the line and going back through the cat's door. I caught him before he discovered the one leading out the back door to the alley, but it's only a matter of time before Trouble shows him. So, we either lock the cat out—or we lock him in, or we'll have both animals out roaming the streets."

Colby crossed the room and picked up Tink, then took him and showed him the cat door. Tink couldn't concentrate on anything but the scary teddy bear lying right in front of the escape hatch.

"No going out that door, okay, pal?"

He set the dog down and it scrambled away, darting under the couch, where it huddled for a couple of minutes before peeking out.

"Looks like we might get some rest, after all. Too bad the big bad teddy bear wasn't on guard the other night when you had the break-in." Which reminded him. He'd have to get that shade put back up tonight. He didn't like the idea that anyone could walk by on the street and peer into Becca's shop.

Maybe a yappy dog wasn't such a bad idea. The mutt might be scared of a teddy bear, but he'd earn his kibble if he would alert them to strangers on the premises.

Chapter Nine

Colby had had such high hopes for his organizational skills, had thought for sure he could pass them along to Becca and make her life a bit easier. After all, they were older now, more mature. Surely she'd see the merits of doing things his way.

Well, that was a pipe dream. Between the cat stealing from the neighbors, the dog yapping and chasing the cat and knocking over stuff, the customers who came in just to hang around instead of buying stuff, and Becca's skewed view on things that totally opposed his, Colby was at his wit's end.

Each morning he started his day with good intentions and ended up feeling as though he'd been agitated in the washing machine, whirled through the dryer and, for added good measure, cranked through an old-fashioned clothes wringer.

He doubted he resembled anything close to a high-powered corporate attorney. A *partner,* for crying out loud.

He kicked the dryer door closed—not because he

was irritated, but because his hands were filled with clean laundry. Good thing he wasn't one of those bachelors who didn't know how to do all this domestic stuff.

As for Becca's skills, now those were in serious question. She could cook, he'd give her that. Laundry, organizing and picking up after herself were whole other matters.

He'd been at Becca's almost a week. The sheriff didn't have any leads on the break-in, and Colby still held the possibility in the back of his mind that the intruder might well return. He hoped to God he was wrong.

If not, he hoped to God he'd be here to protect her. He couldn't stay forever.

Today they were going to get another set of X-rays on her hand and have her stitches checked. He could tell she was still in some pain, so he didn't hold out hope that the doc was going to tell her she was well and free to kick up her heels.

And for some reason, that made him feel better. Not that he wanted her in pain. But if she could do everything for herself, he would no longer be needed—meaning, he wouldn't have an excuse to stay with her.

Which was a double-edged sword for sure. He had no business wanting to stay. Yet he was like a man beating his head against the same brick wall, trying to pass through a restricted area where he certainly didn't belong.

In Becca Sue Ellsworth's life.

He rounded the corner into her bedroom and stopped dead in his tracks. The door to the bathroom was wide open and Becca stood in front of the mirror, examining the bruise on her side.

She was wearing blue bikini underwear and a matching tank top, which she'd pulled clear up to the underside of her breast. The bruise that covered her from armpit to hipbone had turned ugly shades of green and purple.

Colby clenched his teeth, willed his libido to settle. He wasn't sure which was stronger—his anger that she'd been hurt, or his desire for this crazy, annoying, beautiful woman.

"It's a wonder the bastard didn't break your ribs."

Becca shrieked and jerked down her top. "Colby! I'm in my underwear."

"I can see that." He moved farther into the room. "If the pile of dirty clothes next to the washing machine is anything to go by, underwear is about the only thing you've got to wear."

She pulled a towel from the rack and held it in front of her.

"Forget the modesty, sugar pie. I think we're past that." He set the stack of clothes on the sink counter, unfolded a pair of capris and held them out. "Step in."

"I can do that myself."

"I imagine you can. But why spend half an hour and get all frustrated when I can have you in your clothes in just a couple of minutes?"

Becca Sue nearly choked on a breath. Colby

Flynn offering to put her *in* her clothes rather than taking her out of them took some getting used to.

With her heart pounding and her cheeks flaming, she marched over to him and braced her good hand on his shoulder, then put first one foot, then the other into the pants legs. She could smell the shampoo in his hair as he bent in front of her, then straightened up, tugging her capris over her thighs. She gave a little shimmy to ease the material over her hips, and wondered if she'd gained weight with all this inactivity.

"Did you dry these on the hot setting or something?" she asked.

"Hush up, darlin'. Your body's as dynamite as ever."

She sucked in her stomach as he reached his arms around her and pulled up the zipper at the back of her pants. She hadn't been fishing for a compliment. But the one he'd so easily tossed out gave her a thrill.

And so did his fingers as they lingered against the small of her back.

She could feel his breath stir the hair at her temple. His knees bumped hers and all it would take was a tiny step and they'd be pressed together from toes to chest. Lord, she wanted to take that step.

She looked up, met his hazel gaze. He winked. "I'm glad you took my advice and wore a tank top instead of a bra. That bruise on your side is nasty."

He stepped back and picked up a sleeveless, button-front shirt.

Great. He knew darn well she couldn't manage buttons.

And why wasn't he as hot and bothered by this dressing ritual as she was?

She threaded her arms through the sleeve openings, then stood like a tin soldier as he buttoned the front, his knuckles brushing the inside swell of her small breasts through the thin material of her tank top. She could feel her nipples grow hard and was glad that the cotton shirt hid the sight from him.

"We've got about twenty minutes before we have to leave for your doctor appointment. You going to make it?"

She glanced in the mirror, saw that the ends of her hair had gotten wet in the bath. Other than that, she thought she looked okay. Was he seeing something she wasn't?

"Now that I'm properly clothed, I think I can manage it. Why? Have I forgotten something I'm supposed to do?"

"Not that I know of. I just figured if you were going to do the makeup thing, you should get a move on."

"I've already done my makeup." Granted, she'd used a light hand and she hadn't put on any lip gloss, but did she look bad? "Are you saying I need more?"

"No. Never mind." He backed out of the bathroom. "I was just making conversation. I'll go feed the animals."

Becca scrutinized herself in the mirror.

Conversation, my foot.

She checked just to make sure she'd applied mascara to *both* eyes, determined that she had, then swiped the lip-gloss wand over her lips and slid her feet into her sandals.

She heard the cat and the dog strike up a fuss, and Colby's voice right in the middle of things.

She was starting to get too used to the sound of his voice in her home. And that was dangerous.

THEY WERE RIGHT ON TIME for her appointment, stopping by the radiology department for an X-ray before they made their way back to Dr. O'Rourke's office and settled in the mauve-cushioned chairs.

"Are you sure I look okay?" Ever since his comment on her makeup, she'd felt out of sorts.

"Sugar pie, if you looked any more enticing, I'd want to eat you up."

She jolted and tried not to put another connota- tion on that remark. "So, how come you said what you said about my makeup this morning?"

"Man, I'm sorry I opened my mouth. I didn't have sisters, so I'm not real tactful in that department."

"We lived together, Colby," she reminded. "You've got some experience."

"Yes. And you wore more war paint on your face back then."

"Was that good or bad?"

"Neither. You looked great. But I like the more wholesome, subtle look you have now."

"Wonderful. I've always wanted to look whole- some. Good old Becca Sue. The girl next door."

"Make that the girl across the street."

"Split hairs if you want. Wholesome is not going to get me the grand passion of my life that leads to family and happily-ever-after."

He shifted sideways, propped his arm on the back of her chair and toyed with the hair behind her ear.

"Sugar pie, from a man's point of view, wholesome is sexy. Especially packaged the way you are. You've no worries in that department."

What about with you? she wanted to ask. *I don't see you jumping in with any offers.* But just then, the nurse called her name.

She stood, and Colby stood with her. At first she thought he was just being a gentleman. But when he followed her to the door leading to the examining rooms, she paused.

"Um, I can do this by myself."

He shook his head and grinned. "Sorry, sugar pie. I don't trust you to tell me the details."

"What if I have to get undressed?" she whispered, aware of the nurse several feet away, waiting patiently.

"I'll step outside or turn my back if it'll make you feel better."

Unable to stall any longer, Becca turned and smiled at the nurse, then followed her to the treatment room, acting as though it were perfectly fine that Colby Flynn was trailing behind like an entitled husband or lover.

They got the preliminaries out of the way: blood pressure—slightly elevated. Pulse rate—a bit fast.

She'd already stated that she wasn't pregnant and listed the date of her last menstrual period for the X-ray technicians, but had to go through it all over again with the nurse. Didn't anybody talk to each other in doctor's offices or share notes?

When the nurse left, promising the doctor would be in momentarily, Becca glanced at Colby. He was slouched in a chair in the corner, grinning at her.

"What?"

"No need to blush like a schoolgirl. These are perfectly natural questions."

"Yeah, well you're not exactly one of my girl-friends sitting there, you know. I find it *un*natural to speak about such subjects with my *ex*-boyfriend present.

"Hmm. I've been thinking of myself more in terms of a lady's maid." He grinned. "Ex-boyfriend does elevate me on the masculinity scale."

She was about to ask him what was with this masculinity thing all of a sudden—the man had no problems in that department—when Lily O'Rourke swung through the door. Her long, red-gold hair was swept up into a loose bun that looked soft and stylish, and set off her classically beautiful features.

"Becca, my goodness, I heard about the break-in." Lily laid aside the chart and hugged Becca, her professional gaze sweeping over each visible injury. "I'm sorry I wasn't on call last Sunday. I did talk to the emergency doctor and he filled me in on the details."

"Don't worry about it. I was treated really well."

Lily had been several years ahead of Becca in school, but as it was in small towns, everyone knew everyone else's business and most were considered good friends. Lily was high on Becca's list of friends.

Lily glanced behind her and raised an eyebrow, clearly surprised by Colby's presence, then reached out and shook his hand. "Hey, Colby. I didn't expect to see you here."

"I'm staying with Becca Sue."

"On the couch," Becca interjected, then shrugged when Lily glanced up from the chart.

"Darlin', I don't think Dr. O'Rourke is judging us."

"Not as long as you're not messing with Becca Sue's emotions, I'm not." Lily said the words pleasantly enough, but there was an edge of warning.

Colby felt that wolf-and-Red-Riding-Hood syndrome again. "I'm just helping out at the store and stuff. She's a bit handicapped. And she's not the easiest patient. Doesn't want to take the pain meds, doesn't want to wear the sling."

Lily laughed. "Okay. I like you. You can stay." She took the latest set of X-rays over to a lighted box and flipped the switch. Colby joined her, staring at the injured bone.

Becca, sitting on the examining table, wasn't close enough to get a good look, but even if she had been, Colby and Lily were hogging all the space.

She ought to be getting used to people acting like she wasn't in the room. Sure, it was sweet of Colby to take such good care of her, to be worried about her, but that sort of behavior messed with her emotions.

It made her yearn for an eternity of tomorrows.

Made her forget that theirs was a no-strings-attached series of yesterdays.

Dr. O'Rourke turned from the X-rays and spoke to Becca. "You've got good bones. This one's already knitting back together, so I can't see any reason to put a cast on. The splint is doing a fine job of keeping the hand and wrist immobile. Another couple of weeks and you should be able to go without even that."

"Cool. What about showering? I've been going over to Donetta's to have my hair washed. Even in the bathtub, though, it's such a pain trying not to get this thing wet."

Lily examined the stretch bandage that the X-ray tech had rewrapped around the splint. "You've done a really good job of keeping this clean. You should see how gross some of these look after a week." She plucked some supplies from an overhead cabinet, then began to unwrap the bandage on Becca's splint.

"Colby's made sure I haven't lifted a finger so that it *could* get dirty."

"Good for Colby. You can remove the splint to shower and bathe if you want. I'm going to put on a smaller, cuter model. Those emergency docs seem to think one size fits all and tend to go hog-wild with the wrapping." She rolled her eyes at the hard fiberglass contraption that went clear up to Becca's elbow. "I'll also send you home with some fresh bandages to rewrap the splint. You can probably manage it yourself.

"And, if you can't get it comfortable or tight enough," Lily added, giving Becca's arm a soft pat, "you can come back in and my nurse will wrap it for you."

"I imagine I can handle it," Colby said.

Lily nodded but didn't comment. Becca wondered if the doctor was thinking the same thing she was—how long would Colby be around to handle it?

"Is my hand supposed to still hurt when I bend my fingers?"

"That's normal. It's only been five days, Becca. Don't rush the healing. Now, let's have a look at these stitches." She gently removed the gauze and tape from Becca's head.

Colby stepped up right next to the examining table, having a look himself.

"Nothing like being on display," Becca muttered. "I feel like a lab specimen."

"Hush," Colby said, wincing when the gauze stuck to the stitches.

Becca couldn't stop her laugh. "Why are you wincing? It's *my* forehead."

"Reflex reaction."

Like men having labor pains along with their wives? Becca wondered. Criminy. She wasn't Colby's wife, and a few stitches weren't childbirth.

Lily used a cotton ball soaked in something wet to

loosen the gauze and pulled it off without another hitch.

"Looks good," the doctor said. "Nice even stitches. A couple have already started to dissolve. You'll have a small scar, but your bangs will cover it." She cleaned the wound. "I'm going to leave the bandage off. Don't rub or pull at these stitches. Let them dissolve at their own pace. I might need to snip the knot, but we can do that next time you come in."

"Can I wash my face, or get the area wet?"

"Gently. Pat dry."

Becca felt silly asking so many questions, but she'd never in her life had stitches or a broken bone or a bruise the size of a skein of yarn across her side.

"I'd like to check your ribs, too." Lily glanced at Colby, then at Becca, her gesture a silent question.

"It's okay. He's seen it." That very morning, in fact.

Lily nodded, then pulled up Becca's top and the tank top she wore beneath it, being careful to preserve her modesty.

"Swelling's gone down. Bruise is looking normally nasty." She probed the side and Becca winced. "Sorry. I know it's still tender. You're very lucky you weren't injured more badly. I'm still stunned that someone broke in and did this to you. Did they steal much?"

"Nothing, actually."

"Then what in the world…?"

Becca shrugged.

"We think we might have interrupted him before

he had a chance to bag anything," Colby said. "I'm hoping he wasn't looking for something specific Becca Sue might have picked up at an estate sale."

Becca was momentarily startled by this line of reasoning. Colby had been asking her about recent estate sale purchases, but she hadn't put two and two together. Why would she? It had never been a problem in the past.

No wonder he thought the intruder might come back. She'd almost convinced herself that he was being overcautious because he saw so much crime in his daily work as an attorney. But those had all been cases outside of Hope Valley.

She shivered slightly. She didn't want to be afraid in her own home, in her own business.

Lily lowered Becca's top. "Well, in either case, it's good that you're not staying alone for a while. Keep taking the pain meds as needed and finish up the antibiotics that were prescribed."

"What about the sling? Can I leave it off?"

"I suppose. Try to wear it as much as possible this next week, though. You'll probably find that you'll ache more if you don't wear it. Just use your good judgment. The sling also helps to keep you from bumping the bone, so if you're walking around without it, be very careful. Come see me in two weeks—sooner if you have any questions or need help wrapping the splint."

Lily left the room, and Colby helped Becca scoot off the examining table.

In another two weeks—when she had her next

appointment—Colby would probably be gone. He'd already told her he was only in town for three weeks—and the first week was almost over.

Becca put the sling back on just to make Colby happy, and they left the doctor's office.

By the time they got back to her shop, Trouble was nowhere in sight, and neither was the dog. Evidently the guard teddy bear was doing its job where Tink was concerned.

"I think we better check the animals before we open for business," Colby said.

In the apartment, they found Tinky-Winky sitting in the middle of the kitchen floor, the contents of the trash can shredded next to him. He was doing his best to ignore the mess beside him, as though he hadn't had a single thing to do with it. Probably wanted to blame the cat—who was perched in the window by the fire escape, staring at the humans and looking bored.

"I thought Sunny said he was a 'good little dog,'" Colby complained, glaring at the pooch. Tink shivered as if on cue.

Colby cleaned up the mess, noting that the pint-size animal followed him around like an adoring teenager. It had even snuggled with him on the couch last night when he'd been sure it would have wanted to sleep with Becca. After chasing the cat and being scared silly by the teddy bear, Tink had reversed his thinking, and now ran from the cat, jumping into Colby's arms for protection.

"Have you found a place to live in Dallas?" Becca asked.

"Not yet." He was surprised by the change of subject.

"Aren't you cutting things a bit close?"

"I imagine I'll be pretty busy getting settled at the office. I can stay in a hotel or rent a furnished condo until things ease up."

"What about Tinky-Winky?"

He frowned, nearly stepping on the tiny animal as it danced around his feet. "What about him?"

"You'll need to make sure the place you rent accepts animals."

"Who said I'm taking him?"

"Sunny gave him to you!"

"I didn't ask her to." He pulled out a chair at the kitchen table and sat. Tinky hopped into his lap.

Although he tried to act uninterested, his hand automatically went to steady the tiny animal, lingered at its thigh, his thumb stroking.

Damn it. He had a sneaking suspicion that Tink already had his heart wrapped up and tied with a bow.

Just like the woman sitting across from him.

THE PHONE RANG at 3:00 a.m. Colby shot up off the couch, dumping the dog in the process. Tink barked once, then jumped back up on the blankets and curled in a ball. Colby was astonished to see that the cat was draped on the arm of the sofa within inches of the dog. Since when had the animals called a truce?

He snatched up his jeans and stepped into them,

heading toward Becca's room as the phone stopped ringing. She was standing next to the bed.

"Okay. We'll be right there," she said.

"What?" he asked when she disconnected.

"Sunny's in labor."

"In labor or had the baby?"

"In labor. But it's close."

"Who called?"

"Tracy Lynn."

"Why didn't she wait until the baby was born? It's 3:00 a.m., for crying out loud."

Becca gave him a look that suggested he had the IQ of a gnat.

"Would *you* want to go through labor without your friends?" She went to the closet and snatched out a pair of yoga pants, a tank top and a hooded, lightweight jacket that went with the set.

"Thankfully, I'm not a woman and I'll never have to make that decision." Automatically, he helped her get her pants pulled up—they had an elastic waist, so it was an easy task. She didn't even balk when he held the tank top for her, helping her slip her head and arms through.

"Darn it, I'll never get this splint through the sleeve of this jacket. Maybe I should just take it off."

"Slow down there, sugar pie." He tested the stretchiness of the sleeve, then bunched up the material and pulled the opening wide. "I think the smaller splint might make it. Give it a shot."

She threaded her arm through, and he pulled the

cuff all the way to her elbow so that it completely cleared the splint.

"Ye of little faith," he murmured and picked up the blue sling. When she opened her mouth to argue, he cut her off. "You're going out in public and you don't want to bump into anything."

"Fine." She ducked her head through the opening, and slid her arm into the fabric cradle. "If you're going with me, you better hurry up and get dressed."

"I can only handle one of us at a time. Sure you don't want to wait until morning and visit at a reasonable hour?"

"You're welcome to go back to bed. I'm going to the hospital to help coach my friend through labor. I've done it with Donetta and Tracy Lynn, and I'm not missing out with Sunny."

"Okay, okay. Give me two minutes to grab a shirt and shoes."

It took a bit longer than two minutes to dress and brush his teeth. Tink had his head poked out of the blankets, watching Colby's every move.

"We'll be back," he promised the little dog. "Keep my spot warm. I have a feeling we're all going to need a nap."

He swiped a loaf of banana bread out of Becca's well-stocked freezer and zapped it in the microwave for a few seconds. He figured it would be thawed by the time they got to the hospital. No sense in starving to death while waiting for a kid to be born. He plunked a plastic knife in his T-shirt pocket and met Becca at the door to the top of the stairwell.

It took only half an hour to get to the hospital just outside Austin. Since the hospital doors didn't officially open for several more hours, they entered through the emergency entrance and Becca led the way to the elevators, pushing the third-floor button once they stepped inside.

"Guess you've done this a time or two."

"Us Texas Sweethearts stick together."

Hmm, he thought. Three of the Sweethearts having babies. No wonder Becca had kids on her mind.

The atmosphere in the waiting room felt like a hometown reunion. Storm and Donetta were there, their baby asleep in her car seat. Tori, Sunny and Jack's seven-year-old daughter, sat next to the baby, watching it sleep. Tracy Lynn had her arm linked through Donetta's, and Linc—who was holding his and Tracy's sleeping child—stood next to Storm. Suddenly Anna rushed into the waiting room from another entrance and began excitedly telling the others what was going on in the labor room, and that Jack was as pale as a ghost.

Becca left Colby's side the moment they crossed the threshold and went to her girlfriends. Colby shrugged, sat down on one of the couches and set the banana bread on the table in front of them, noting that someone had brought a deck of cards.

"I brought food," he said.

Storm and Linc immediately joined him. Jack came into the room, and he *did* look as bad as Anna had said.

"What are you doing in here?" Becca said to Jack, her voice filled with censure. "Who's with Sunny?"

Jackson Slade stared at her for a moment, clearly in a daze, then turned on his heel and headed back the way he'd come.

Colby chuckled. "He's a ball of nerves."

"Poor guy," Linc said. "It's hell watching your wife go through that kind of pain and not being able to do anything for her." Linc looked up at Tracy Lynn, then down at his sleeping daughter. "Tracy Lynn didn't want any drugs, wanted to do everything natural. About brought me to my knees."

Donetta laughed. "I, on the other hand, was begging for drugs the minute they got me in a gown."

"Hollering, was more like it," Storm interjected with amused indulgence.

"And Sunny?" Colby asked.

"Oh, she's being a martyr," Donetta said. "Thinks she can drop this kid like her cattle patients drop their calves. You just wait. She'll be chasing that epidural guy down the hall before long."

"She might choose to have her child as nature intended," Tracy Lynn said, a hint of her high-society primness bleeding through her Southern drawl.

Becca laughed. "Let's go find out firsthand." She hooked her good arm through Tracy's and together the three women headed toward the labor room. Anna stayed behind since she'd been in with Sunny already.

The time seemed to drag by, but Colby under-
stood why Becca had been so adamant about being
here. The bond of friendship between these women
was something else. He envied it, even. He didn't
have close friendships like this. Oh, sure, he was
friends with Linc and Jack and Storm and a bunch
of other guys in town, but not best pals like Becca,
Donetta, Sunny and Tracy. What they had was
special.

The three women were in and out of the waiting
room for the next six hours, laughing over who'd
had the best advice for Sunny and who'd made her
the maddest. Sunny had given in and taken the
drugs, and was able to sleep some, allowing Jack to
relax and get some color back in his face.

They played several hands of poker, and when
Becca anted in to a game, Colby had to hold her
cards for her.

He felt an odd twinge at his wrist, wondered if
he were having sympathy pains. All these husbands
talking about feeling their wives' pain must be
getting to him.

He pulled at the stretch band of his great-grandfather's watch, rubbed the skin beneath it. He
couldn't tell if the skin itched or hurt.

The thought that he could somehow telepathi-
cally share the pain of Becca Sue's injury was ludi-
crous. He could just see himself using that argument
in a court of law. The judge would likely fine him
for contempt and lock him up for his own safety.

At ten o'clock the next morning, Storm, Linc,

Colby and little Tori were left alone in the waiting room with the two babies. Becca, Donetta, Tracy and Anna were in the delivery room with Sunny and Jack. Colby had never realized hospitals let so many people in to witness a childbirth.

A few minutes after ten, Becca Sue came rushing through the door, tears on her cheeks. "It's a boy! Jackson Dwight Slade Jr. has entered the world, weighing in at nine pounds, four ounces."

Storm whistled. "That's a big boy. How's my sister doing?"

"Happy as a cow in clover," Becca reported.

"I wouldn't be making any cow analogies if I were you," Storm commented with a grin.

"I can make them," Becca said with a laugh. "Just you guys can't." She moved over to Colby and sat down, snatching up the last crumbs of banana bread.

Donetta and Tracy Lynn came back in, fairly dancing with excitement. "Oh, he's so cute," Donetta said. "Good thing he didn't stay in there to cook any longer. Can you believe? Nine pounds, four ounces!"

"Bigger than a bowling ball," Tracy added.

Colby winced. God almighty, he didn't even want to think about the image that conjured. Ouch.

They all sat down, and Colby started to wonder what the plan was. The baby was here, so shouldn't they be headed home?

No one seemed interested in leaving, and he was just about to ask, when Jack came into the waiting room, grinning like a small dog with a big bone. He hugged Tori, then hugged everyone else in the room, including Colby.

"Y'all want to come see my new son? They let me watch while they gave him a bath and did all sorts of unkind things to him, but he's all warm and wrapped up and in the nursery now."

Becca jumped up and pulled Colby with her. She fairly floated down the hall. He could almost feel her excitement.

Once they got in front of the glass partition, though, standing apart from the other couples, she seemed to go all sad on him. She touched the glass with her fingertips, the yearning in her eyes almost too intense to watch.

Again he thought of her tears and the plea in her voice seven years ago when he'd told her he wasn't the man to give her what she wanted and promised her she would someday find that right man and have the family she deserved.

But what if it doesn't happen? The words echoed in his mind.

Damn it. Why did he keep feeling pangs of guilt? As if it were *his* fault she hadn't found her dream.

He lightly touched the wispy bangs at her temple, and felt his gut sting when she turned her lovely green eyes to his.

Oh, man.

"You really want this badly, don't you?" he asked softly. "Babies and family."

"I don't know why that should surprise you. It's

all I've ever wanted—and the reason you broke up with me."

He looked away, because she was right. That had been a big part of their split.

What she had wanted—marriage, babies, commitment, promises of forever—had scared him spitless.

It still did.

Because failure wasn't an option he allowed in his life. At least not when it came to relationships and commitment.

And he simply couldn't guarantee that any committed vow of forever he made would stick. That something wouldn't go wrong in the day in, day out nature of a marriage that might turn love into hate.

Chapter Ten

As they stood there outside the hospital nursery, Becca grappled with her emotions.

During the years she'd been building her business, she'd been able to put her dreams of family on the back burner. The desire for children hadn't been such a big deal until her friends had begun to marry and experience the joys of coupledom, pregnancies and motherhood.

Of the four Texas Sweethearts, Becca had been the one who'd wanted family the most—or at least for the longest time. She'd come from a relatively big family, two happily married parents and four kids—her three older brothers and herself.

Then an accident on the highway had taken the lives of her parents and brothers. Becca had stayed home that weekend while the rest of her family had taken their motor home on a trip to Las Vegas in celebration of her brother Ben's twenty-first birthday.

She still felt guilty that she hadn't gone. Maybe

her presence would have caused them to be on the highway at a different moment in time. She might have taken longer to get dressed, or needed to stop at a restroom, or won a jackpot in Vegas and had to wait fifteen extra minutes for her payout.

Two minutes or fifteen minutes might have made the difference. They wouldn't have been on that particular stretch of highway at 10:00 p.m. when a Jeep full of high school seniors had been passing a string of cars around a blind curve in a No Passing zone.

The highway patrol said Becca's father hadn't had a chance to take evasive action. The head-on collision at sixty-five miles an hour had sent the motor home off the road and into a ball of flames.

In mere seconds she'd lost her entire family.

The life insurance had helped her to start Becca's Attic, but she would have given up the business in a heartbeat just to have her family back.

She shook herself out of the awful thoughts.

Now, her store was her tribute to her family—to their history that dated clear back to the Alamo, to the traditions that had been handed down through the years, the recipes and knitting patterns, and to her parents' love of books and antiques. Nearly every item in her store had roots, had meant something to someone. By caring for them, finding them new homes, she felt she was adding substance to the family lives of her customers.

But she'd never given up hope that she would start a family of her own someday. Have lots of children who would grow up and give her grandbabies to tell stories to, to carry on the legacy of the Ellsworth bloodline.

At one time, she'd been sure that the man standing next to her gazing into the nursery window would be her husband.

How wrong she was. She'd known, all those years ago, that he'd desperately tried to let her down easy—heck, that was the reason he'd made his drunken offer to help her have a baby if she didn't find Mr. Right by the time she turned thirty.

She'd certainly tried, but none of the relationships had worked out. In Hope Valley, available men were either just passing through or she'd known them since grade school and couldn't work up the spark to see herself settled down with them and being happy for the rest of her life.

She wanted grand passion.

The kind she'd had with Colby.

"We should probably get going." Becca turned away from both Colby and the newborns and went over to her friends, hugging them all goodbye.

The trip back to Becca's apartment was silent. She noticed the muscle working in Colby's jaw, the white-knuckled grip he had on the steering wheel.

He was probably getting ready to run for the hills.

Teasing and dancing around the subject of having babies was one thing. Confronting the issue head-on in all seriousness was quite another.

Becca figured he was spooked but good.

When they entered through the back door of the store and went up to the apartment, the dog and cat jumped up to greet them. Well, at least Tinky did. Trouble tried to act all macho, as if he hadn't just been cuddling with the little dog.

Despite the tension Becca had been feeling, she smiled when Colby automatically bent down to pick up Tinky.

"Looks like these two are becoming pals," she said, walking over to stroke Trouble's soft black fur. The cat swished his tail and purred. Then, obviously deciding he was too cool for the display of affection, he jumped off the sofa and relocated himself next to the fire escape window. The torn screen beyond the window was proof that Trouble didn't understand why he couldn't have the metal landing as his own private patio.

Colby didn't comment on the animals. He still seemed tense.

He sat on the sofa, settled the dog beside him. Tink jumped into his lap again.

Becca was starting to feel unnerved by Colby's odd silence. And the intensity of his stare. "Why are you looking at me like that?" she finally asked.

"How come you don't date?"

Where had that question come from? "I have."

"You should be in a serious relationship by now."

"Right. What am I supposed to do? Go snag some stranger off the street and say, 'Hey, come be my man'?"

His eyes narrowed. "You're gorgeous, Becca Sue. Maybe you're just really picky when it comes to men."

Was she? Probably. She'd set her standards based on Colby. So far, no one had measured up.

"You know," she said, "you're making me feel bad here. I'm not crazy about being alone and single. I'd love to have what my friends have. But between work and this being a small town and the lack of available men, the love bug hasn't seen fit to cross my door."

"I don't mean to make you feel bad, Becca." Colby said the words softly, gently.

"Then why are we talking about this?" She kicked off her shoes, then realized she'd have to put them right back on. She needed to go open the shop.

"Because it tears me up to see the way you look at those babies. You were meant to be a mother."

Becca shrugged and looked away, felt her eyes sting. She'd spent many years and many nights wondering what was wrong with her that she couldn't find a relationship. Couldn't find the happiness that comes with knowing you've met your soul mate.

And it wasn't as though she was the picky one and had done all the dumping. She'd been dumped a few times, too.

Most memorably by the man sitting across from her.

"What about artificial insemination?" he asked. "Have you considered that?"

"Sure. But it's too expensive."

"Adoption?"

"I haven't looked into that yet. As far as I know, I'm perfectly capable of carrying a baby in my own womb. I want that experience, too, if at all possible."

"Do you want to try to have a baby with me?"

Her stomach and heart lurched at the same time, sending a jolt of adrenaline through her veins that made her hot and dizzy. It was a moment before she could find her voice. "What are you suggesting? That you're suddenly ready for family life?"

He studied her for a long moment before he shook his head. "This would be for you, Becca."

He was offering sex. His sperm. That was all.

"Right. We've got two weeks, and I've got stitches and a gimpy arm. I'm sure that inspires a good deal of lust in you."

He continued to stare at her, not speaking.

Criminy, he was really serious.

She'd been consumed with the thought of having a baby for weeks…months…maybe even years, and had usually cast Colby in a starring role. But that had been fantasy, not real life.

Having it suddenly become real flustered her. The thought of hopping into bed with Colby Flynn, making love—no, having sex—with him again after all these years, well, that took some thinking about.

She leaped up from the sofa, slid her feet into her shoes. "I need to go open the store."

He nodded and stood, surprising her when he let the subject drop.

Lord have mercy. This conversation changed everything, took away any ease she'd begun to build over Colby spending his days and nights with her.

He was protecting her until he felt assured her intruder wasn't likely to return or until he had to move to Dallas, which ever came first. But who was going to protect her heart?

Now, as there'd been seven years ago, a deal was on the table.

And by dog, she was really tempted to take it.

AFTER COLBY had dropped his bombshell question, they spent the rest of the afternoon and the next day walking on eggshells around each other.

Colby would give a person the shirt off his back if they needed it—or in her case, his sperm.

On Sunday morning, they went to church, then stopped by the hospital to visit Sunny. She was scheduled to go home the next day, but since they let the babies stay in the rooms with the moms, Becca got to hold Jack Jr. Taking off the sling, she was able to comfortably cuddle the baby boy and kiss his soft round cheek.

"I'm your Auntie Becca," she crooned. The baby puckered his little lips. "Oh, yes, you recognize my voice, don't you?"

Colby watched her like a hawk.

She knew what he was doing and why. She could have kissed him for his caring. But by the same token, she resented his hovering. The smile she wore on the outside wasn't quite as bright on the inside.

And the very fact that he watched her this way made the question he'd asked yesterday remain smack-dab in the front of her brain.

Do you want to try to have a baby with me?
Lordy.

Donetta breezed into the hospital room. "I might have known Becca would be hogging that baby. Hand him over."

Becca gave a mock glare and transferred baby Jack into Donetta's waiting arms. The baby began to fuss.

"See there?" Becca gloated. "He was doing fine with me. Clearly I have the touch."

"Well, he'll settle down for Aunt Donetta."

Sure enough, Jack Jr. closed his eyes and relaxed.

"Did Colby get to hold him?" Donetta asked.

Colby held up his hands. "I'm good. Figure the little guy needs a break. You all keep passing him around like a football and he's going to be sore."

"Where'd you hear that?" Sunny and Donetta asked at the same time.

"Yeah," Becca said, "Mr. Baby Expert."

Colby shrugged. "I believe it was your mother," he said to Sunny, then looked at Donetta. "Who's also your mother-in-law. I passed her in the hall when I was coming back from the restroom."

"Oh," Sunny said with a shake of her head. "She only said that because she wanted Jack Junior all to herself."

Tracy Lynn walked in the door. "Is there a party going on? I can hear y'all talking clear out in the hall. And I happen to think that it's true about babies getting sore. How would you like to be passed from pillar to post?" She reached out her arms and Donetta automatically transferred the baby into them.

Becca laughed. "Good one, Tracy Lynn. You just said you think the child's going to get sore and you go and grab him."

"Honestly. I didn't grab. Besides, he loves his aunt Tracy Lynn."

The nurse popped her head in the door and made a shushing sound.

Since she and Colby had been there the longest, Becca decided to head out. "We're going to take off, Sunny. Is there anything you need?"

"No. I'm good. How about you? I see you have on a smaller splint. I didn't even get a chance to hear what the doctor said."

"The bone's healing itself. Should be out of this thing in a couple weeks."

"Cool," Donetta said.

"Anyway, we're off." Becca gave hugs and kisses all around, then scooted out the door with Colby right behind her.

When they were outside, the hot afternoon sun had heated the asphalt, causing it to stick to the bottom of her sandals. Every step felt and sounded as though she'd stepped on a lollipop without its wrapper.

Becca was glad she'd worn the short sundress in anticipation of the day's heat. The blue sling hadn't exactly made a fashion statement with the spaghetti straps and flowered green material, and she'd been glad of an excuse to take it off in the hospital room.

She kept waiting for Colby to hound her about putting it back on, but he didn't.

"Let's take a ride out to my place," Colby said as he helped her into the truck.

"Sure." She checked the bottoms of her shoes before she got in, surprised they weren't coated with black tar, then tossed the sling on the floor along with her purse.

Since it was Sunday the shop was closed, and frankly, she was glad for the break. She'd set her days off to coincide with her friends' schedules, as well as the town's. Donetta's beauty salon brought Becca a lot of business. No sense staying open when most everything else on Main Street was closed.

Despite her insistence to remain open all last week, Becca occasionally closed the shop on Mondays when she could talk Tracy Lynn or Donetta into poking through antique stores, or yard and estate sales with her. Sunny wasn't much of a shopper, preferring to stick to animals.

Now that Sunny had a baby to care for, Becca imagined she'd be quite reluctant to go back to work. Sunny had already brought in a veterinarian friend of hers from California to fill in while she was on maternity leave. Becca hadn't yet met the guy.

The air-conditioning in the truck blew on high, pulling the scent of alfalfa and fresh-mown grass through the vents as she and Colby traveled out of town. The summer sun was bright and the birds were plentiful in the evergreen trees, occasionally swooping across the road in front of the truck.

The farther they got from town, the lighter Becca felt. She hadn't realized how cooped up she'd been feeling lately. Having the full use of only one hand sure put a damper on her active life.

Colby turned off the main highway onto a gravel road that snaked around for about a quarter of a mile before the house came into sight.

It was as beautiful as Becca remembered, a white, two-story structure with green shutters and an old-fashioned wraparound porch, sitting on six acres adorned with lush shade trees and a peach orchard. A creek meandered through one side of the property, and a pond she'd swam in as a child occupied the other.

"Wow. That's quite an antenna you've got on the roof," she said, not remembering the McGivers having that when they'd lived here.

"It's for my ham radio."

"Ah." She remembered now that he'd had his ham license since he was a teenager. When they'd lived together that summer, their apartment hadn't been conducive to the long-range communication setup, and he'd often talked about the hobby and how much he missed it. "At least you've got plenty of room—no close neighbors who'll get annoyed with your antenna messing with their television reception."

"Yep. Another plus for living in the country."

Yet he intended to move to the city, she thought. She couldn't imagine how he could bear to part with the place.

"This was the McGivers's place," she told him. "Arlene McGiver was my Sunday school teacher."

"Ah," he drawled. "The Sunday school teacher who gave Maizy to Grandma Lee?"

"One and the same."

"Small world."

"Everything looks pretty much the same—although maybe not quite so big."

He pulled the truck to a stop by the front door. "Funny how things seem so much larger through a child's eyes. A while back I drove by the house I lived in as a kid, and it didn't look any bigger than a one-room cabin. I mean, as a kid I knew we didn't live in a big place, especially compared to other people's houses, but I sure didn't realize it was that tiny."

"Do you ever hear from your parents?"

"Hell no."

She reached out and laid a hand on his forearm, felt the hardened muscles under his warm skin. "I'm sorry."

"Nothing to be sorry about. The estrangement suits us all just fine."

"Are you so sure, Colby? It's been a lot of years."

"And it'll be a whole lot more—forever, as far as I'm concerned."

"Someday don't you think you'd want your children to know their grandparents?"

His features were totally serious. "No, Becca, I wouldn't. I would never subject a child—or anyone I cared about—to people who have difficulty being civil for any length of time, and who think nothing of rejecting those who try to get close to them."

"Maybe they've changed."

"Sugar pie, you always did want everything wrapped up and tied with a shiny red bow. Life doesn't always work that way." He got out of the truck and came around to her side to open the door for her. "Subject closed," he said before she could continue the conversation.

"Okay. Sorry I brought up bad memories. It's just—"

He stopped her with a finger over her lips, then stunned her when he bent down and replaced his finger with his mouth, giving her a kiss that was as gentle as the breeze, as reverent as if she were a princess.

"I know, sugar pie," he said when he lifted his head. "You miss your family and can't understand why anyone with kinfolk *living* would keep their distance."

She nodded.

"You were one of the lucky ones," he said as they headed for the house. "Not everyone has what you had. Sometimes it's better to cut the ties rather than to try to mold the dysfunction into something resembling a relationship. Otherwise, everybody ends up miserable."

They mounted the porch steps and she trailed her hand along the smooth white wood of the railing, letting her eyes feast on the surrounding landscape as she grappled with her emotions and the lingering tingle from that unexpected kiss. A lawn-mowing tractor sat in the side yard, the grass around it shorter than the sod on the other side of the driveway. This was a lot of ground to keep up, and she wondered if he mowed it in sections.

Just then, she realized that something was missing.

"You don't have a For Sale sign up."

"No. I haven't listed it. You want to come in out of the heat?" He held open the front door and she walked through.

The interior was warm and a bit stuffy, since it had been closed up for the past week. As far as she knew, he'd only been back here long enough to pack a duffel bag. The rest of the time, he'd been at her place.

He moved over and fiddled with the thermostat. "The air will kick on in a sec. Doesn't usually take long to cool down."

The foyer was wide and deep, its floor a medium-stained hardwood that flowed up the stairs and throughout the rest of the house. Beautiful crown molding and wainscoting adorned the walls, both surfaces painted contrasting shades of white, the ivory on the wood making the walls look the color of butter from one angle, and cream from another.

Straight ahead was the living room, and beyond that the kitchen. As they moved farther into the house, Becca recognized some of the personal items Colby had had when they were together.

"Hey. You still have that painting." Above the mantel over the fireplace was an oil rendering of a house on a lake done by a once-obscure artist whose work was becoming quite popular.

They'd bought the painting at a garage sale seven years ago—well, Colby had bought it, but she'd been with him. And it had hung in *their* apartment. She'd been really annoyed that he'd taken it when he'd left.

"You know, that's probably worth some money now," she said.

"I didn't buy it for the art value. I just liked it."

"Have you noticed that the house in the painting looks a lot like this place?" She moved closer to the framed canvas, while Colby went into the kitchen. She could hear him opening and closing cupboard doors. Although the art depicted a farmhouse on a small lake, Colby's house and its pond could easily have been used as the model.

Is that why she'd been so drawn to the painting all those years ago—because it stirred up fond memories at the McGivers's farm? She hadn't made the connection then, at least not consciously.

Colby came up behind her, reaching around her with a glass of sweet iced tea. "I guess they do look a lot alike," he said.

She took the glass from him, followed him over to the sofa. Not a single cushion or magazine was out of place. "Have you even *started* to pack?"

"Nope. Planned to, but I ended up staying at your place."

She'd intended to leave a cushion's space between them, but he snagged her elbow and guided her down next to him. Tucking her close to his side, with her back to his chest, he positioned a throw pillow in his lap and propped her arm on it.

"Thanks." Her heart was beating like a bongo drum at the closeness of their bodies. First that breezy kiss, now this nonchalant cuddling.

She cleared her throat. "You don't seem too worried."

He shrugged. "I won't need much the first month or so that I'm there. Be mostly working. Besides, if I need stuff, I can call in some movers and have them pack up."

"For a man known to cross all his *T*'s and dot every *I*, you seem awfully blasé about moving."

He toyed with her hair, easing her head back against his shoulder. "It'll get done when it needs to."

"I'd have probably started packing a month ago."

"You anxious to get rid of me or something?"

"No." *Just the opposite.* "I guess I'm just surprised, and trying to get a bead on you." Without thinking, she kicked off her sandals and swung her legs up onto the couch. As soon as she'd done it, she froze. Snuggled against him this way, should she really be getting even more comfortable? Was she sending out weird signals?

He rested his cheek against the top of her head. "Relax."

"I am."

She felt him smile. Then he asked, "So, where'd you sleep when you spent the night here all those years ago?"

"In the yellow room upstairs."

"Mmm."

"Do you still have a yellow room?"

"Want to see?" He leaned sideways and looked at her.

"Sure."

He helped her sit up and stand, then, keeping his fingers entwined with hers, he led her toward the stairs.

Why did she suddenly feel as though she'd agreed to more than a tour of the upstairs?

There were four bedrooms upstairs and Becca went straight to the corner room, delighted to find that it was still yellow—and still had the same queen-size bed with its white, cast-iron head and foot rails, the same creamy quilt and the yellow cushion in the window seat. She remembered sitting there often, gazing out at the meandering creek.

"Did you buy this place furnished?"

"Not totally. The McGivers were downsizing, didn't need four rooms of furniture, so I negotiated for some of it."

"I always loved this quilt," Becca said, running her fingernail over the fine stitches surrounding the buttercup design.

"I hardly ever come in here. It's a whole lot of house for just me."

"True. What made you buy it?"

He shrugged. "I liked it and I could."

She glanced at him, not really surprised by his answer. He'd hated the fact that he grew up poor, so buying something just because he could made a certain amount of sense. Clearly he hadn't chosen the place with the idea of filling it with a wife and kids. He'd already made that clear enough.

"Come on. I'll show you the rest."

He opened the other two bedroom doors so she could poke her head in, pointed out the bathroom as they passed, then led her to the master bedroom at the opposite end of the hall. This room, too, had a wonderful window seat, but it looked out over the pond and the peach orchard.

Here, he'd made changes. The room was more masculine, with heavy oak furniture, a satin bedspread in burgundy and gold and a sculpted wool rug that picked up the same colors. There were no photographs on the dressers, but the knickknacks and accessories around the room made it feel homey and lived-in.

Becca could easily imagine that with a few feminine touches, this room would be the perfect retreat for relaxing…and loving.

"What do you think?" he asked softly.

She looked into his eyes, and had a feeling that he was asking about more than her opinion on the decor.

She took the chicken route and answered, "It's nice."

His hand came up slowly, cupped her cheek, his fingers tunneling through her hair. Watching her, giving her plenty of time to object, he began to lower his mouth to hers. The anticipation was so excruciating, Becca stood on tiptoe and closed the last breath of distance herself.

Her arms went around his neck. She tried not to clobber him with her splint, then forgot all about her injured hand and everything else as he shifted and took the kiss deeper. She opened her mouth, invited him in, tasted the sweet tea on his lips and tongue. Moaning, she pressed closer, wanting to climb right up his body.

Oh, this was what she remembered. The fire. The passion.

One thing about Colby Flynn—he could kiss like nobody's business.

At last he broke the contact, raised his head, his breathing as hard and fast as hers.

"The timing's right. I calculated it when you told the X-ray tech the date of your last period. Be sure, Becca Sue."

His words momentarily snatched her out of the sensual fog.

Do you want to try to have a baby with me?

She licked her lips. "So you planned this…today? You didn't just suddenly get swept up with lust?"

"Hell yes, I got swept up." A crease formed between his eyebrows. "Do you think I'm just doing you a service? Because if you do, sugar, think again. I want to make love with you so badly I'm about three seconds away from total combustion. I just needed to know that we're on the same page— because I wasn't planning to use any means of birth control."

Becca felt a moment of panic. Could she do this? *Should* she do this?

He was offering up her dream—a child—with no strings attached. If she wanted those strings, then it was a no go.

Becca had known for a long time that she'd never fallen out of love with Colby Flynn. He was her greatest weakness and her heart's every desire.

The fact that he would do this for her made her love him even more. They'd done a good job of staying friends over the years, even after an intimate relationship and a bittersweet breakup.

Oh, she knew full well there would be another bittersweet parting, but baby or not, she was confident that they could still remain friends.

Colby would always be part of her life.

And that's what made up her mind.

If a baby came out of their union, she was fully prepared to be a single mother. After all, if she'd had the means, she would have already started the process of becoming a single mother by choice.

Colby was offering her an alternative. A means to her end.

"We're on the same page, Colby. I want to make love with you."

Chapter Eleven

Colby unzipped the back of her dress, eased the spaghetti straps from her shoulders and slid them down until the dress fell in a puddle at her feet.

She wore only a pair of white bikini underwear—and a huge bruise on her side. He bent down and softly kissed the discolored skin.

"I hate that this happened to you."

"Shh."

She took his face, brought it back to hers, wrapped herself around him like a honeysuckle vine and poured so much passion into her kiss that his knees went weak. Man alive, he'd forgotten what this woman did to him.

She wasn't a shy lover. She took what she wanted with avid, greedy hands and mouth and no apologies. She was every man's fantasy—and he was the lucky sucker who was making love to her.

He lifted her off her feet, kissing her, strode to the bed and placed her on the satin bedspread. He yanked off his T-shirt, toed off his shoes and slid down next to her on the bed, making sure her injured side wasn't against him.

The satin was cool against his bare skin, a sensuous contrast to the heat of Becca's body. He wanted to feast, to map every soft, exquisite inch of her, refresh his memory of all her feminine secrets and delights. But he was damned afraid he'd lose control and forget that her body was tender in places.

"I don't want to hurt you."

"Well, I don't want to hurt you, either, but I might if you don't hurry." She whimpered, rolled into him, pressed her hips against his.

He nearly laughed. Man, he'd missed this woman.

He swept his hand over her breast, the curve of her waist, her hips, then rolled with her until she was lying on top of him.

And all the while he kissed her.

He thought he could be content with just kissing Becca Sue. She had a mouth made for loving and she knew how to use it.

She was the only woman who could make him forget his own name. His hands cupped her bottom, pressed her harder against his groin.

"Take off your pants," she said against his mouth, grinding her hips into him, undulating, first in slow circles, then faster and faster. "I'm burning up, Colby. I need more."

He reversed their positions, tucked her beneath him, then slid down her body, pulling her panties down and off. Spreading her legs, he kissed her with the most intimate kiss a man could give a woman, using his lips and his tongue and the barest pressure of his teeth to bring her to a climax. Her hips bucked and she cried out, snatching at his hair, trying to pull him up her body, knocking him in the ear with her splint.

"I'm sorry," she panted, practically crying. "Come to me. Now."

He tore off his jeans, then sank between her legs, holding the top of his body off hers, and pressed against her femininity, feeling her wet heat surround the tip of his penis. He nearly lost it right then, like a teenager with his first girl.

Slowly, carefully, he entered her, pressing forward by inches. He gritted his teeth, felt her warmth wrap around him like a skin-tight glove, felt the immediate spasms as she shot upward into another swift climax, her body squeezing him, milking him, driving him mad.

He wanted to make it last, but the strength of her orgasm drew him right over the edge, and with a powerful thrust, he slammed into her hard and fast, again and again, feeling his seed pumping into her. Sensations shivered through him and he thought they'd never stop, didn't know this kind of pleasure could last like this, drugging him, exhausting him.

And Becca's body was keeping right up, throbbing, pulsing around him like a lover's heartbeat.

It *was* a lover's heartbeat, he realized.

His lover's.

As the last of his seed spilled into her, he had a single coherent thought.

Did we make a baby?

BECCA WAS EXHAUSTED, but it was the very best kind of tired. The air-conditioning whispered over her heated body, cooling her.

So many familiar things, she thought. This man beside her, this wonderful farmhouse, the incredible lovemaking they'd just shared.

When they'd been together before, sex had been the one constant between them, the best part of their togetherness. It had been when they were out of bed that they'd butted heads. His organizational habits and her lack of them. The fact that they'd both wanted control. They'd never learned to walk *beside* each other. Instead, each had raced to take the lead.

Why hadn't one of them compromised? she wondered.

Perhaps things might have been different if they'd come to the relationship as the people they were today, more mature, more sure of life and love and what they wanted.

But therein lay the biggest flaw in her reasoning. Their wants were still nearly a state apart.

She wanted children.

He wanted the job in Dallas. And very likely, a woman named Cassandra Wells. A woman who was climbing the corporate ladder just as he was, who wouldn't have the time or interest in diapers, first steps, the tooth fairy, ballet lessons or T-ball.

In light of that, it seemed stupid that she'd even agreed to make love with him. Then again, there were no guarantees she'd get pregnant before he had to leave.

Was she perhaps, deep down, hoping that the renewed sexual intimacy between them would make him realize it was *her* he wanted?

"You okay, sugar pie?"

His whiskey drawl jerked her out of her musings. Darn it, she would *not* think about another woman while she was naked in bed with Colby.

"Mmm," she murmured, tracing the line of his sternum with the tip of her finger, following it down his flat stomach, then back up. Goose bumps rose on his skin. "That was very nice, thank you."

He chuckled, shifted to his side and propped himself up on one elbow so he could look down at her. "Very nice, thank you?"

She grinned. "Is it the 'very nice,' or the 'thank you' that has that little crease forming between your eyebrows?"

"Depends. What are you thanking me for?"

"The orgasm, of course." She felt him relax— as she'd intended. This aftermath of lovemaking could easily become awkward, and she didn't want it to.

"I seem to recall there was more than one."

"Okay, the *orgasms*," she corrected. "You're such a stickler for details."

"Yep." He kissed her neck, nibbled at the lobe of her ear. "And thank *you*."

"Not bad for a woman with a handicap, huh?" She raised her splinted arm.

"Not bad, indeed. Though you managed to clobber me with it a couple of times."

She laughed. "Sorry. I love a slow-talkin' man with a slow hand, but you were being a little *too* slow."

"Is that so?" He traced his tongue down her neck, over the swell of her breast, swirled it around the pebble of her nipple. "Too slow like this?"

"Um…no, that's pretty good."

He sucked the nipple into his mouth, leisurely slid his palm down the center of her flat belly, pressing low on her abdomen. "How about this?"

She arched her hips, trying to urge his hand farther down. "You're stepping into the danger zone."

He trailed his fingers back up her body and she nearly cursed him. "Try not to start something you don't intend to finish," she said, her mind already glazing over at the erotic skill of his touch.

"Oh, I intend to finish it." He lightly stroked her arm, grazed the underside of her splint, danced the pads of his fingertips over hers. "So try to keep this weapon right where it is, because I felt a little rushed last time. I'm aiming for a stronger description than 'very nice,' and I'm thinking it might just take the rest of the afternoon."

He was as good as his word, making love to her again and again clear through to the evening.

Becca ran out of praiseworthy descriptions.

A WEEK LATER, on Saturday, Becca watched Colby as he bent over a shelf of journals. He was frowning as he pulled them off one by one and set them on the floor of the shop.

They hadn't stayed the night at Colby's farm-house last Sunday because Tink was home alone with Trouble—a scary prospect. As it turned out, the animals had survived each other quite well.

Although she and Colby had made love too many times to count over the past six days, Becca was glad that their first time after all these years had been at the farmhouse. She couldn't exactly say why. It was just something she felt in her bones.

Perhaps because the incredible memory would be etched on her brain forever. When it came time for him to leave, she wouldn't be left alone surrounded by the familiar walls of her apartment, confronted with that powerful image.

Oh, she'd have plenty of powerful memories now that he was sleeping with her in her bed.

Just not that particular one.

It was becoming clear that Colby was no longer staying with her as a protector. She'd already chalked up the break-in to a random act that she'd inadvertently interrupted. And though her hand still wasn't up to the task of kneading bread dough, she was able to do most everything else without help.

"How come you've got all these journals?" Colby asked as he pulled another stack off the shelf. "Why would anyone keep these things, let alone buy them?"

"They're pieces of history," she said and crossed

to join him. "The lives of women—and sometimes men—and what they went through. Who they were and what their dreams were." She took a thin, leather bound book out of the stack, opened it and scanned the cursive handwriting.

"This woman's husband is off fighting the war." She skimmed farther down the page. "Ah, he's fighting for the South. Good man."

"Spoken like a true Texan," Colby teased.

"Darn right." She skimmed farther. "Everything is so vivid. She's writing about the crops in the fields and the difficulty keeping them up, the pies she baked that day, and the vegetables she canned. And…oh."

"What is it?" At her stunned tone he immediately moved closer, tucked his arm around her waist.

"She had to bury her baby boy." Tears stung Becca's eyes, and she looked up at Colby.

"What happened to her baby?"

"He died of scarlet fever. She dug the grave by herself because her husband wasn't there."

Colby leaned forward and kissed her temple. "See? Now I *really* don't know why you'd want to collect stuff like this. It's sad."

She smiled at him, her emotions settling. "But it's interesting, too. Think of that woman's strength, the steel in her backbone. She didn't throw herself in the grave with her child or run off to her psychiatrist's office. She did what had to be done, and then she brought in the corn from the fields."

Becca closed the journal and ran her fingertip

lovingly over the cracks in the leather. "You know, you and I both have ancestors that date back to the Alamo. I'm always looking for connections, long-lost pieces of my family tree."

"And mine, too."

She nodded and smiled at him.

"I'm sorry you lost your family, Becca. And I'm sorry I wasn't here for you."

She didn't really want to talk about this. She'd still been reeling from their breakup when her parents had asked her to go to Las Vegas with the family to celebrate her brother's birthday.

She'd soon gotten a double whammy—the loss of Colby, and the forever loss of her family.

She shrugged. "Thanks. I know it was a long time ago, but it still feels like yesterday. I miss them every day."

"Is that why you collect journals?" He toyed with the hair at her nape. "Looking for relatives?"

"Not really. I mean, I like to know where I came from. What my ancestors were like. It's exciting when you find a connection. Like that watch." She touched the gold band encircling his wrist. "When I saw D. J. McGee inscribed on the back I just knew this was your great-grandfather's. I remember you told me once that he was special to you."

"Yeah. Great-grandpa Dan. I was hardly old enough to remember him, and the fact that I do—so clearly—means he made quite an impression."

"What about your grandparents?"

"I guess they knew better than to be around my

folks. I didn't see much of them. My great-grandpa Dan made the effort, though. Don't know why. Can't ask him now."

"Oh, don't be flip."

"I'm not. But this is all history, sugar pie. I'm a guy who likes to live in the present and future."

"I do, too. But there's nothing wrong with revering the ones who came before us, who fought for us and paved the way for the luxuries we now enjoy." She held up her hand before he could argue.

"Your parents aside. Criminy. Don't toss out all the apples just because a couple were bad."

He cupped his hand around the back of her head, drew her forward and kissed her. His lips were dry and warm, and so very clever. They made her forget where she was, her name, even.

The bell over the front door jingled. Instead of releasing her immediately, Colby leisurely finished the kiss, slowly drew back, his gaze holding her as effectively as the hand still at the back of her neck.

"We have a customer," she whispered, unable to look away from the heat in his hazel eyes.

"Mm-hm. And they can't see us because we're behind the shelves."

"But they'll find us in a minute."

He pressed his lips to hers once more.

"Colby!" she whispered against his mouth. "We have to see who it is."

He grinned against her mouth and gave her one last, quick kiss. Straightening her top—even though he hadn't made a single attempt to divest her of it—she rounded the bookshelves and pasted a smile on her face.

An older man with gray hair peeking out from beneath his trucker's hat smiled back.

"Can I help you with something?" Becca asked.

"Naw. Just looking. This your store?"

"Yes. I'm Becca Sue Ellsworth." She waved her splinted hand as an apology for not offering to shake hands.

"Whoa, had an accident, huh?"

"Mm." She didn't want to scare off the customers telling them how she got hurt. She noticed the man was looking at the jewelry by the front counter. She didn't want to hover—she hated it when salespeople did that to her, especially if she truly were just poking around.

So Becca busied herself behind the coffee bar. "We've got coffee and bakery items back here if you're interested. Holler if you need anything or have questions."

"Thanks. The wife might like one of these brace-lets, but I think I ought to send her in to look for herself. Returns everything I buy for her and ex-changes it for something else."

Becca laughed. "Don't take it personally. My mother was like that, too. And she loved my daddy to pieces."

"Glad to hear it. Still…" He abandoned the brace-lets and began to browse the greeting cards. Pretty soon, he waved and left the store. She saw him walk next door to the saddle shop. Probably making his way toward Donetta's where his wife was having her hair done.

Colby had poked his head around the shelf, obviously realized he didn't know the customer, and had gone back to work putting the journals in chronological order. In that particular area, she appreciated his organizational tendencies.

She'd been meaning to go through all the journals and put them in order, but invariably she got caught up in reading them and ran out of time. Thus, there were stacks of them in all shapes and sizes, and no easy way to tell which were the oldest, or which belonged to the same family.

She thought about his comment of living in the present and future. He certainly did a lot of that. His cell phone had rung more than usual this past week. She'd overheard some of the conversations, a case coming up having to do with an oil company violating EPA restrictions, and a few people calling for representation, only to be told that he was closing up his business.

Every time she turned around there were reminders that he was leaving.

Yet he still hadn't begun to pack.

She didn't want him to move, but his lackadaisical attitude on this point was driving her nuts.

Just then, Tink raced around the corner, dragging a stuffed elephant that was almost as big as he was. She noticed that Colby immediately stopped what he was doing to play tug-of-war with him.

Lord, she was as attached to this little dog as if

she'd raised it from a pup. And so was Colby, which meant he would no doubt take Tink with him when he left.

No wonder she was so fond of history. This anticipating-the-future stuff was the pits.

She hated knowing what was coming. Because as much as she was prepared for it, she knew it would involve heartache.

Chapter Twelve

Colby felt his frustration mounting—both at himself and at the world. The three-week departure date he'd originally settled on had passed a week ago.

Every time he thought about leaving, something would come up that Becca needed help with, and he'd convince himself she couldn't operate without his help.

He wasn't normally a man who lied to himself, and he wondered when the hell he'd developed the bad habit.

Steven Wells had been understanding so far. But Colby didn't imagine the man's good humor would stretch many more days.

He propped Becca's cinnamon roll recipe against the flour canister and lined up the ingredients. He'd baked several batches of these suckers over the past few weeks, but they never quite came out the same as when Becca made them.

Miz Lloyd and Trudy Fay Simmons had been kind enough to point that out to him. Bless their little old hearts.

They should come stand here kneading this dough for five long minutes, then sit around for ten minutes waiting for it to rise just so they could flatten it out again, doctor it with goodies, and roll it up in a coil only to wait *another* twenty minutes for it to rise some more before it could be baked.

Colby glanced at his watch. 8:00 p.m. Man, he was beat. Walking in Becca Sue's footsteps these past weeks made him truly appreciate her and all that she managed to do—the myriad of details involved in running her store during the day and baking at night, and she still made time for friends. Amazing.

Right now she was chatting on the phone with one of her girlfriends. If he hadn't been in here doing the baking, he imagined she'd be enjoying the phone call *and* baking.

That would be beyond his capabilities.

He was also beginning to realize that there was an odd sort of order to Becca Sue's disorganization. She was an excellent businesswoman—smart, friendly and charming, with an eye for what would appeal to her customers.

He'd found out within a few days that his idea of putting all the china together in one spot didn't work. He'd made that one sizable sale only because he'd been holding the merchandise when Norah Conway had come in. If it had been grouped with all the rest of the stuff, it would have blended in and possibly been overlooked.

That was Becca's theory. And maybe she was right. Her placement of her merchandise was based on shrewd business sense, and he was learning to bow to her superior knowledge.

He couldn't remember ever learning so much about—and from—a woman. Or wanting to. Yet, each day he made new discoveries about Becca, indeed anticipated them.

The more they made love and spent time together, the more Colby feared that seven years ago, he'd let the best thing in his life get away from him.

But damn it, he was still terrified of commitment. Of failing. And hurting her.

She'd let him off easy all those years ago, still remaining his friend. He'd believed it was because he'd broken things off before something bad could go wrong, before the spats and disagreements turned into an all-out war that would make them hate each other.

Like in his parents' relationship.

That sort of devastation, the bitterness and utter failure of something that had begun with good intentions, scared him to death.

He glanced again at his watch, which was sprinkled with flour. He'd been kneading this dough for three minutes and already it felt like thirty. He still had to clean up his mess and...

Spying the one-quarter cup of sugar still sitting on the counter, he swore.

"Grandma Lee said you should never swear in the presence of bread dough. Makes it tough."

He nearly jumped, hadn't heard Becca come in. "I bet Grandma Lee never forgot to put in the doggone sugar."

"Mmm. That'll tend to make a body mad—especially when you get all the way to this stage before you remember."

"I hate it when I don't get things right the first time." He fisted his hands in the dough, needing to strangle something.

"I know. You should loosen up. That attitude'll send you to an early grave." She moved up beside him, casually put her hand on his back, stroking, massaging…petting. He didn't think she even realized what she was doing. It was the sort of gesture a lover would use…or a loved one.

Man, he was turning into a real sap.

"What now?" he asked. "Do I scrap the project and start over?"

"No. We'll just serve reduced-calorie cinnamon rolls tomorrow. Or you can compensate and add more brown sugar and butter between your layers."

"If I do that, I can't mark them as reduced calorie, can I?"

"Probably not."

"I just know Miz Lloyd's going to stop by tomorrow. I think she marks on her calendar which days I bake these rolls and only buys them so she can tell me they don't measure up to yours."

"Of course she doesn't. I'm well known in these parts for my cinnamon rolls. You wouldn't want to steal my thunder." She snitched one of the raisins he'd measured into a glass dish, and grinned when he shot her a frown.

"That was Sunny on the phone," she said. "Beau's

barbecuing steaks tomorrow and they want us to come over for supper." Beau had been the number-one cowboy on Jackson Slade's ranch for nearly forty years, but these days he spent most of his time in the kitchen, bickering with Cora Harriet over who got to use the stove and take care of the housekeeping chores.

"Sounds good," Colby said. "Means I don't have to cook."

"Oh, you poor thing. You're so overworked," she teased. "Linc and Tracy Lynn, and Storm and Donetta are invited, too," she continued. "After supper we girls are going to fuss with the babies and you guys are supposed to see who can bankrupt the other in a hot and heavy game of poker."

"Mm. I always wanted to take some of Linc's money away from him. Ought to be easy pickings. I'm better at poker than he is."

She laughed. "Don't be bragging and telling him that. You guys'll end up in a pissing contest, and we'll be there all night."

He covered the bowl with a clean dish towel and set the dough aside to rise.

It occurred to him that they were talking like a married couple, but he couldn't seem to work up a decent worry over it. Especially with Becca Sue standing here fresh from a bath, wearing thin summer pajamas and smelling good enough to eat.

"I'll be subtle." He scooped her up against his chest. "Right now, though, we've got ten minutes. Wanna neck?" He gently closed his teeth over the sensitive area between the side of her neck and shoulder.

She shivered and laughed. "I thought you'd never ask."

THE NEXT EVENING, Becca walked into Sunny and Jack's living room, surprised to see all the guys huddled around the game table looking at each other's cards.

"What kind of poker is this?" she asked. "Did somebody forget how to play and the rest of you are teaching him?"

None of the men answered. They all stared intently at Colby, who was staring at his antique watch—which was on *Storm's* wrist.

My gosh. Had Colby bet his watch, an heirloom, and lost it to Storm? Surely Storm wouldn't keep something that personal. After all, this was supposed to be a *friendly* game of poker.

Colby flicked out a card and it landed on the table facedown.

"I think it was three longs and a dit on the left side," Storm said, "and a little dit on the right."

"King of hearts," Colby said, then flipped over the card on the table.

King of hearts. Okay, Becca thought. They've gone from poker to magic tricks.

He dealt another single card—facedown.

Storm studied the watch.

"Boy, you're slow as molasses in January," Beau complained.

Storm shot the older man a silencing look. "I'm trying to figure it out. I'm not as quick at reading code as Colby is. I think that was a dash and a dot on the left, and two dots on the right."

"Five of diamonds," Colby said.

He flipped the card over and sure enough, it was the five of diamonds.

"Man, that's incredible!" Linc said. "A person could make a killing with this at the casinos. How's it work?"

"I'd say there's some sort of computer chip in there," Storm said. "It's mind-boggling what they can program into those tiny chips these days." He passed the watch back to Colby.

"Could be along the lines of sonar," Jack added. "Bouncing off the table and onto the card. If you know the code and are fast enough at it—"

"Or like them optical scanners in the grocery stores," Beau said, shaking his head. "Who in tarnation would come up with something like this?"

"What in the world are y'all talking about?" Becca asked. By then, Donetta, Tracy Lynn and Sunny had joined her.

Colby pulled her down to sit on his thigh, handed her the watch and positioned her fingers against the back of the case, then picked up the deck of cards.

"Keep it low to the table," he said, then tossed out a card, which arced upward before landing on the table.

Becca nearly dropped the watch. "What in the world? It shocked me."

"No, it's not shocking you." He tossed out another card.

She felt the sensation again. "It is, too!" She jumped up from his lap and dropped the watch on the table.

"I think it's more of a vibration-type impulse," Colby said. He fished a knife from his pocket, flipped over the watch and proceeded to take it apart.

Becca gasped. "What are you doing? That's an antique heirloom."

"With a value that's obviously higher for a certain type of wearer. I thought these things on the back were screws," he said, prying the case apart. "But apparently they're nodes that send out a code every time a card is tossed on the table."

"You mean you've been wearing that watch all this time and it's been shocking you?"

"Not all the time. See this extra stem?" He paused and turned the watch so that everyone at the table could get a look at the side of the case before he flipped it back over and continued his effort to pry off the back.

"I never could figure out what it was for— thought maybe it had to do with setting the second hand and just didn't work. I realized tonight that it's when I mess with the stem or bump it that I feel the sensations. The first time I really noticed it was at the hospital when Sunny was having the baby and y'all were playing cards. I didn't know what was going on. Tonight it was driving me nuts."

He probed around with the knife, and the rest of

the men leaned forward, all of their heads practically touching as they tried to see what Colby was doing.

"I learned Morse code in military school when I was a kid, and I've kept up with it through my years of ham radio use," he said, clearly for the benefit of the others in the room.

"So this watch is talking to you in Morse code?" Tracy Lynn asked.

"Similar. It's sending short and long impulses, like dits and dahs. The left node is transmitting the card, ace, two through ten, jack, queen, king. Ace is a dit, two is two dits, three is three, four's a dah—a longer impulse. Five's a dah plus a dit, six is a dah and two dits, eight would be two dahs, nine two dahs and a dit, and so on."

Becca was fairly good at math, but Colby was reeling off the code so quickly she really had to concentrate.

"The right side was harder to figure out, but it seems to be tapping out the suit. Hearts is one dit, diamonds is two dits, spades is three and clubs is four. With practice, I imagine a person could get pretty good at distinguishing the two sides and feeling the sounds."

"*Feeling* the sounds?" Becca asked.

"Terminology. That's how we learn code— through sound."

He was truly enjoying this, Becca thought. And so were the rest of the men. What was it about probing into the innards of something, be it an engine or the workings of a watch, that would draw the attention of every guy within seeing or hearing distance?

"Apparently," Colby said, "my great-grandpa Dan's watch is a high-tech cheating device." He glanced up at Becca. "There goes your theory about any redeeming ancestors in my family tree."

"Colby, your great-grandfather has been dead for a lot of years. There's no telling who's had this watch in the meantime."

"Probably got passed down to my old man. I told you he was always looking to win at the lottery or at cards."

Becca stepped back to give him more room to ruin the watch. Besides, Jack, Linc, Storm and Beau were all breathing down Colby's neck.

"There it is," Colby said at last, pointing to a tiny part with the tip of his knife. "I'll bet that little gizmo is a computer chip."

The men studied the insides of the watch. Becca couldn't tell one part from the next.

"I'll see that bet," Storm said, "and raise you one. I'm betting this here card reader is what someone was after the night they broke into Becca's shop."

Colby nodded thoughtfully. "The timing's right. Becca gave me the watch the week before the break-in. It might have taken that long for the owner to track down who'd bought it."

All the men turned to Becca.

"Do you remember what estate sale you bought the watch at?" Storm asked.

"Actually, I found it at a pawnshop in Austin.

And I'd had it about a week before I gave it to Colby."

"Why didn't you tell me you'd bought it at a pawnshop?" Colby asked.

"You didn't ask. Besides, I gave you the watch as a gift. I'm not in the habit of telling someone where I bought their gift. You're the one who assumed I'd picked up something at an estate sale that someone wanted back."

"A pawnshop does make more sense," Storm said. "Chances are, the guy expected to get it back out of hock before it was sold."

"Or maybe it was stolen from him," Becca said. "And that person hocked it, thinking it was just a regular watch."

"I doubt it," Linc said. "If it was stolen, the watch's owner wouldn't know to go to the pawnshop and harass them into giving out the name and address of who bought it—which is what I'm thinking might have happened. I'm sure if we pay a call to the pawnbroker we can get a little information of our own."

"Of course this is all speculation," Storm interjected. "The break-in at Becca's could have been totally random."

"Ha!" Donetta said. "And pigs'll be flying down Main Street in the morning."

"Thank you, sweetheart, for shooting down my attempt to stop a group of well-meaning vigilantes."

"Well," Tracy Lynn said, "at least we're well-meaning. Right, girls?" She looked around, and Becca, Sunny and Donetta nodded.

"I was referring to the *men* in the room," Storm said, raking a hand through his hair.

Becca nearly laughed. Her girlfriends were as fierce as any group of men.

"I'd like to remind all of you that this is a law-enforcement matter," Storm said, and held out his hand for the watch.

Colby passed it to him.

Donetta scooted next to her husband. "Ooh. I just love it when he goes all Texas Ranger on us."

"That's Sheriff, darlin'. Let's keep our departments current."

She gave her husband a sassy wink and they all laughed.

"I'll go get you a plastic bag so you don't lose any of them little parts," Beau said, getting up from the table.

Becca was distracted, still staring at the open watch case. She had the name of the pawnshop in her files at the store. It wasn't a place she frequented. She'd been passing by, seen the shop and gone in on a whim, coming out half an hour later feeling as though the trip had been pure synchronicity.

Because she'd found a piece of Colby's past.

And it had given her an excuse to contact him.

In the end, she'd chickened out and mailed it to him—all the way across the street, for crying out loud. And he had thanked her by mail as well.

Now look at them. Sleeping in the same bed, under the same roof.

All because of a watch. And a drunken promise.

Both of which had been given with no strings attached.

That pretty much summed up their relationship.

Colby's light touch at her shoulder brought her out of her thoughts.

"You okay, sugar?" he asked quietly.

She nodded. "What now? Do you think the pawn-broker will tell us who pawned the watch? Or admit it if he gave out my name and address?"

"I'll check it out," Storm said. "I have jurisdiction in parts of Austin—and buddies in the parts I don't. We'll get some answers." The sudden seriousness of his expression and tone reminded everyone in the room that Sheriff Storm Carmichael, ex Texas Ranger, wasn't a man to be trifled with. "Meanwhile, I'll send this watch to the crime lab. We've got some really sharp techie guys there. I have a feeling, though, that they'll come up with the same answer that Colby has. That this is a high-tech cheating device."

Colby locked his gaze with Storm's. "I'd like to go with you when you pay a call to that pawnshop," he said. "Seeing as it's my watch and likely someone in my distant family responsible for what happened to Becca, I think I've got a pretty strong stake in the outcome."

He hoped to God the cheating crook didn't turn out to be his old man.

Chapter Thirteen

The next afternoon, Becca was practically beside herself waiting for Colby to get back. He'd gone with Storm to Arturo's Pawnshop. Lord, she hoped he didn't get in a fight or anything. Colby was an easygoing guy, but he was really mad about her being injured during the break-in.

Funny, she'd never known before that he had such a protective streak.

She told herself that Storm would keep Colby in line. Darn it, though, if he came back with skinned knuckles, she was going to be very upset.

The back door opened and she whirled around.

"Colby! Why are you sneaking in the back? Let me see you. Are you okay? Did you find out anything? Why—"

He kissed her, then grinned down at her indignant look. "I didn't sneak in. Storm stopped by to see Donetta and dropped me off behind her shop, so I walked the rest of the way—the whole two stores length. And I'm fine. Why wouldn't I be?"

"I don't know. I was worried you'd get in a fight or something."

"I'm a lover, sugar pie. Not a fighter."

She ran her gaze over him, raised an eyebrow. "How come your shirt's untucked?"

He shrugged, reached down and tucked it in. "Must have forgotten when I stopped to use the john."

"Tell the truth and shame the devil."

"There was no violence. Honest."

"Did you find out anything?"

"Yes. Storm has a name. He's tracking the guy down as we speak—well, after he visits for a minute with his wife. Then he'll be on his way to bring the guy in for questioning."

"Is it anyone you know?" She held her breath. Colby had finally admitted to her last night that he feared his father was somehow involved—even if he *hadn't* seen his dad in close to twenty years.

"No. Some guy by the name of Buster Derkin pawned the watch. He wanted Arturo to hold it, but Arturo's assistant didn't know about the arrangement and sold it to you. Derkin wasn't a happy camper when he came back and found his watch sold."

"Did Arturo give Buster Derkin my name and address?"

"Yes, the scum. Told Derkin to go buy it back from you. We know what good old Buster did from there."

"Yes. Why do you suppose he didn't try to come back after his first attempt?"

Colby shrugged. "Maybe because I've been here. Or maybe he was in here long enough that night to satisfy himself that you no longer had the watch and he gave up."

"You could be right. I might have caught him on his way out and he just panicked. Poor guy. He probably had gambling debts and was desperate."

"I can't believe you! Are you actually defending the guy who beat you black-and-blue, broke your hand and caused you to have a permanent scar on your head?"

"He didn't beat me black-and-blue—there were only two blows."

"Becca Sue, your side is *still* discolored. So don't be going all soft, because chances are, you'll have to testify against him."

"How can I do that if I never saw him?"

Colby didn't answer her question. His muscles had gone rigid. He was looking out the front window.

Becca followed his gaze. She saw a tall man wearing a western-cut business suit, snakeskin boots and a wide-brim Stetson getting out of a black Mercedes-Benz. Alighting from the passenger side was a beautiful, statuesque blonde, her hair cut in a sleek shoulder-length pageboy. She wore a pale yellow, summer-weight suit, the skirt hitting several inches above her knees, and high-heeled pumps.

Becca felt a twinge of alarm. Why did it suddenly feel like doomsday?

"Becca Sue, I—"

He didn't finish what he'd been about to say. The bell over the front door jingled. The tall man breezed in with a good-natured, robust laugh and booming voice.

"Thought we'd find you here," the man said. He shook hands with Colby. "Figured we ought to come see for ourselves what the holdup was and see if we could hurry you along."

"Steven, this is Becca Sue Ellsworth," Colby introduced. "Becca Sue, Steven and Cassandra Wells."

"How do you do, young lady," Steven said with a smile and held out his hand.

"Don't squeeze," Colby warned. "She's still healing from a broken hand."

Steven took Becca's hand in his and brought it to his lips, placing a soft, gallant kiss on her knuckles. "Pleased to meet you, Becca Sue."

Cassandra gave a soft laugh. "Daddy's a bit dramatic. How are you, Becca Sue?"

Proving that she didn't particularly care about the answer, she turned to Colby. "Hey, Colby." She leaned forward and lightly kissed his cheek with a familiarity that showed she believed her affection was welcome.

Becca's heart sank.

"D'you suppose we can drag you off to dinner?" Steven asked. "We've got some catching up to do. And I brought the files on the Saturn Oil case."

"I don't know," Colby said, glancing at Becca.

"Oh, forgive my manners. Becca Sue's welcome to join us, if she'd like." Steven smiled pleasantly. So did Cassandra, though a bit more strained.

The woman would make a good politician's wife, Becca thought. Or a high-powered attorney's.

The only one who was clearly uncomfortable was Colby. And she knew why.

This was his ship, waiting for him at the dock. And he was hesitating because of her.

For a while, they'd allowed themselves to get caught up in a fairy-tale world. Intimacy had a way of confusing your emotions, messing with your head.

But Becca was determined not to stand in the way of Colby's future dreams. He'd been totally up front with her, told her flat-out that he couldn't promise her forever. He'd only signed on for three weeks— which he'd ended up stretching to four and a half— hoping to leave Becca with *her* future dream.

She didn't know if they'd been successful, but she'd find out soon.

"No," she said, "y'all go on. I've still got a while before I close up here. And I've got inventory in the back that just came in. Besides, I know y'all have a big case to discuss." She looked at Colby. "Go. I'll be fine."

"You sure?"

"I'm positive. Go." She practically pushed him out the door, all the while hoping he'd choose her over these city people. It was silly, really. Well, she wouldn't show her yearning by so much as a twitch. He was uncomfortable enough.

He was faced with what he wanted out of life, and trying not to hurt her in the process.

That was a joke. She'd known all along she'd get hurt. She was prepared. Had walked into this with her eyes wide open. No strings attached.

She watched the three of them file out the door, kept her smile in place until they were gone. Then, holding on to her emotions by a thread, Becca went into the bathroom. She was about to wet her pants and figured she might as well kill two birds with one stone.

She'd already read the instructions on how to use the home pregnancy kit, so it was just a matter of getting the job done. Then she was going to lock the doors—never mind that it was ten minutes before closing time—and go upstairs to lick her wounds in private.

Or maybe she'd be celebrating.

She'd wanted a child so badly, for so long. Now, though, her emotions were all over the place. She felt like crying. Or hitting someone. Maybe a statuesque blonde with killer legs.

What did Colby see in that woman? She was cold. Boring.

"Great, Becca. You saw the woman for two minutes and now you're judging her personality. You ought to be ashamed. And doggone it, I can't believe I'm peeing on a pregnancy stick while the potential father of my potential baby is off having dinner with his girlfriend!"

She set the stick on the counter, wrestled her capris back up her hips, then froze when she heard the bell jingle over the front door.

Her heart leaped in gladness. Had Colby come back? Decided he'd rather eat dinner and make bread dough with her than hang out with that city girl?

She flushed the toilet, snagged the pregnancy stick and shoved it in her pants pocket with her cell phone and hurried back out to the front of the store.

It wasn't Colby.

"Oh, hi again." She tried to put some professional enthusiasm into her voice even though her heart was sinking like a stone. "You're the one whose wife returns all your gifts," she recalled. "Did you decide to take a chance on one of the bracelets, after all?"

"Not these bracelets." He reached back and flipped the lock on the front door. When he faced her again, there was a gun in his hand.

Becca nearly choked on a breath. Her heart slammed against her ribs. Oh, no. Not again!

Although he'd taken her by surprise, she was wide awake this time. She was not going to end up at the hospital for more stitches or splints or—God forbid—a bullet wound.

"What do you want?" Although she tried to steady it, her voice trembled.

"A watch you bought at Arturo's Pawnshop. Gold band. I think you know which one I'm talking about. It's…shall we say, special."

She pretended not to know what he was talking about. "Special? Are you D. J. McGee?"

His bushy gray eyebrows drew together beneath the bill of his trucker's hat. "Yeah, I am."

"Really?" *Lying sack of bones.* "I'm so sorry. You see, I'm into genealogy and tracing folks' family tree. When I saw that watch I remembered that there was a James McGee who fought at the Alamo—"

He waved the gun at her. "Skip the chitchat. Just give me my damned watch and be done with it."

"That's the thing. I don't have the watch. I sold it to someone else who said his great-grandfather was a descendant of James McGee."

"You *sold* it?"

She nodded.

The man swore. "What'd he look like? The one you sold my watch to."

Becca waved her hand at the gun as though it were making her nervous and forgetful—which it darn well was—and inched back a few feet. "I—I don't remember—"

"Younger than me?" he coached. "About the same height, except with brown hair and a mustache?"

"Yes," she lied, taking another step back. Tink and Trouble were upstairs, and she hoped neither of them would come down to investigate. "I think that was him. I can look up the receipt if you like." She whirled around, intending to get behind the counter, put something between herself and that gun…and get herself closer to the stairs or back door.

"Stay where you are," the man shouted. "Damn it, let me think."

"I was just going to get the receipt."

"I don't need it. I know who came for the damn

thing. Was Macky. He worked for Arturo. I never should've told nobody about that watch. He was just waiting for me to get in a fix. I owe money, had to come up with it somehow. I figured I could win a few hands over at the club, make enough to get the loan sharks off my back and get my watch out of hock. I didn't figure on anybody buying it."

"I'm sorry," Becca said, still pretending she didn't know the watch was a cheating device. "Macky—if that's who you think it was—paid in cash, so I didn't have any cause to question or check his identity to know that he wasn't actually J. D. McGee. I feel bad that I sold your family heirloom to a stranger."

"What are you talking about?" the man said, his attention shifting around the room at the merchandise she had on the shelves.

"The inscription," she clarified, slipping her hand in her pocket. She felt the pregnancy strip and her cell phone. The phone was the flip type and she wondered if she could manage to get it open within the confines of her pocket. "You said you were D. J. McGee."

"Oh. Yeah, right." He snatched a pair of French 19th century Louis XV marble urns off the shelf, then tucked a pair of Napoleon III gilt and bronze lamp bases under his arm.

"Since you took what was mine, I'm taking some of yours."

"Why don't you just find Mr. Macky and get your watch back?"

"Oh, I will. Unless you go squealing to the cops the minute I turn my back."

"I won't. I promise. Just go and we'll call it even between us."

"Right." He shoved over a shelf of books, then another.

Becca froze, wanting to scream but unable to find her voice. The man was insane. She leaped back, looking around wildly for an escape, hoping someone would hear and come investigate. As soon as she thought it, she changed her mind, hoped no one *would* show up.

This maniac had a gun. Luckily, the saddle shop next door closed at three on Fridays, and Donetta's shop was too far away to hear the noise.

She couldn't get her cell phone open inside her pocket to dial out. She made a dash for the back door, but another shelf came crashing down in her way. Trapping her.

She smelled gasoline, watched in horror as he doused her wood shelves and furniture with liquid from a flask he'd had in his jacket pocket.

Oh, dear God.

He opened the front door and flicked a match. "See ya round, toots."

The gasoline whooshed into flames, licking all around her. A small pathway, not yet engulfed, led to the back door. She started to climb over the counter, stopped when she heard Tink barking like mad.

The animals!

Flames were licking up the walls, reaching the ceiling. She changed course, barreled through the stairwell door and ran, screaming for Tink and Trouble.

Chapter Fourteen

Colby couldn't concentrate. Something about that pickup truck they'd passed hadn't set right with him. Steven had wanted to have dinner at Angus Twins outside of town, but Colby had talked them into going to Anna's Café. It was only a couple of blocks from Becca's.

Steven was perfectly comfortable in the vinyl booth, setting his Stetson on the table top beside him. Cassandra didn't appear too pleased. She kept wiping at the table with a napkin and brushing her behind with her hand, apparently to dislodge the crumbs she believed were stuck to her skirt.

Why hadn't he ever noticed that air of snobbery about her?

"So," Steven said, "you estimated you'd be moved in three weeks, but it's been four and a half now. Cassandra and I thought we'd better come make sure you hadn't changed your mind."

"Did you notice that silver pickup we passed? Rusted-out tailpipes. Old guy driving?"

Cassandra arched one perfect blond eyebrow.

Steven chuckled. "Can't say as I did. I'm not really in the habit of looking at folks' tailpipes—"

"That's it!" Colby stood, threw his napkin on the table. "The loud muffler. That's what I heard." Within seconds he was out of the booth and running down the street.

His lungs burned as he leaped the curb, sprinted across Maple and back onto the sidewalk.

He saw the silver pickup, saw the tires smoke, heard the sound of rubber gripping the asphalt as it peeled away from the curb.

He hit the street again, legs pumping. Millicent Lloyd, driving her 1965 Bonneville, nearly mowed him down as she sped around the corner, her boat of a car right on the tailgate of the speeding pickup.

He was two doors away, in front of Donetta's beauty salon, when he saw the flames leaping in Becca's store.

"Fire!" He yelled the word as loud as he could. Hell, the fire department was just up the street. They'd probably hear him. He already had his cell phone out, pressing the button that would connect him to emergency services.

Donetta raced out the door of her salon.

"Get out," Colby yelled. "Get everybody out and stay back."

A vague part of his mind noted her dash back inside, hopefully to obey his directive. If Becca's store went up, this whole block was likely to go.

Margo came on the line since both the fire department and sheriff's department were handled by the same dispatch. "Get the fire department to Becca's. It's burning."

He was running, fumbling with his phone. It slipped out of his hand and tumbled into the gutter. He didn't even notice. The only thing on his mind was Becca.

He reached the glass door of her shop, yelling her name.

Damn it, he wasn't going to lose her now that he'd found her again!

Tires squealed behind him. The sheriff's car. "Check the door for heat," Storm shouted in warning just as Colby was about to yank open the door.

Colby touched the glass, found it warm but not hot—he'd seen movies where opening the door fed the fire, even caused a blast.

"Hold on, man," Storm said, grabbing his shoulder.

Colby jerked away. "Becca's in there. Becca!" He opened the door and yelled her name, took a step farther inside.

The store was impassable. Shelving was knocked over, flames eating at the wood and licking the walls. He'd never get to her this way. There was too much blocking his path. He ran back out, sprinted around to the alleyway door in back.

He was reaching for the knob when he looked up. Becca had one leg out the window at the top of the fire escape, both animals clutched in her arms.

"Thank God." Colby took the metal stairs three at a time and reached the landing just as she cleared the window. "Come on, sweetheart."

With his adrenaline pumping he felt as though he could leap ten feet to the ground, if necessary. He snatched Becca, still holding the animals, into his arms and took the stairs instead, the smell of smoke burning his nostrils.

Trouble was squirming to get down, fear and instincts ruling. They both got scratched trying to hold the cat. Tink shivered and stayed quiet.

At the bottom of the fire escape, Colby set Becca on her feet, took the cat from her, then grabbed her left hand, pulling her with him along the alley. They cut through Donetta's beauty salon, coming out onto Main Street.

A crowd had gathered in the middle of the street between the salon and Becca's store. Donetta, clutching her baby, stood next to Storm. Firefighters were already hosing the interior and exterior.

Colby turned to Becca, took a good look at her and hugged her to him. Hard. The cat yowled and leaped down. Tink still shivered.

"Are you okay?" Colby asked, setting her slightly away. "Are you hurt?"

"I'm fine. He came in right after you left. I was in the bathroom—" She stopped, remembered why she'd been in there. "What are you doing back here? I thought you went out to dinner."

"I passed a silver pickup. I didn't recognize the truck. The guy driving it wasn't a local—"

"He was in the shop last week, looking at the bracelets—"

"I know." They were talking over each other. "I recognized him. It bothered me for some reason. I couldn't put my finger on it. Then I remembered that I'd heard a loud muffler the night you were attacked. This truck had rusted tailpipes—it had the same sound."

"So you turned around and came back?"

"We were already at Anna's."

"Sorry I ruined your dinner."

He pulled her hard against him again. "Don't be stupid." He noted that Steven and Cassandra were standing across the street, farther down. He'd have to go talk to them soon.

The firefighters were doing a good job of stopping the flames. But Colby still had a feeling there wouldn't be much left of her store.

God, he felt bad. That store was her life. Her touchstone to her family.

Donetta finally looked around and spied Becca. She gave a glad cry, passed the baby to her mother-in-law and ran toward them. It was a wonder she didn't break her neck in those platform shoes.

"My gosh, Becca! I thought you were inside!"

Colby stepped back as Donetta, tears streaming down her face, hugged Becca tight. The other women who'd been in the beauty salon gathered around. Cars were showing up—Sunny and Jack, Tracy Lynn and Linc.

Storm had left in pursuit of Miz Lloyd's Bonneville and the pickup truck—presumably driven by Buster Derkin. Colby figured that ought to be one hell of a chase, and lamented that he wouldn't be there to see the takedown—to get a crack at the guy himself.

He'd hear about it soon enough, though.

The circle of support around Becca grew larger, and Colby allowed himself to be squeezed out. He figured he'd better go ease Steven and Cassandra's minds, let them know what he'd decided.

SUNNY HAD TAKEN Tink and Trouble over to the veterinarian's office to keep them out of harm's way. The fire department had left, and though they'd cleaned up, Becca was still wading through a pool of watery ash. She felt a lump of emotion gather in her throat.

She'd sent Donetta and Tracy Lynn home, promising to check in later. All three of her friends had offered her a room to herself and a cool bed to sleep in, and it was only a matter of choosing which one to stay with. She said she'd decide later.

Becca imagined Colby was going to have houseguests of his own out at the farmhouse. She'd seen him cross the street to talk with the Wellses a while ago and now wasn't sure where they'd gone.

Fine. What did she care? *A lot.*

"I'm sorry, Becca Sue."

She jumped. She hadn't heard Colby come up behind her. "Nothing for you to be sorry about. I carry fire insurance, so the building will get repaired. I can buy more merchandise." But she couldn't replace the photographs that had burned, or the wonderful journals. All those were lost.

The lump in her throat grew larger, ached. She wanted to sit right down in the middle of this mess and bawl. But she simply didn't have the strength for that kind of hysteria.

"I feel responsible," Colby said. "It was my family heirloom that inadvertently caused all this."

Becca couldn't say why that particular comment tipped her over the edge, but it did. She'd finally reached her emotional limit. She was devastated, and now she was mad as hell.

"I don't want your misplaced guilt or your sympathy, got that?" she said, poking him in the chest. "And furthermore, I don't want a mere sperm donor. I want the whole damned package. Love. Marriage. Commitment. The ups and downs of daily life. The good with the bad. So what if we argue? Everybody argues."

Her voice was rising, but she didn't care. Nor did she care that it was still several hours until twilight, and should anyone choose to stand outside and eavesdrop, he or she would have no problem hearing *or* seeing them. Bring 'em on, she thought.

"Just because your parents didn't care enough to work through the rough spots doesn't mean that *all* marriages end up on the rocks, and if you can't see that, then you're an idiot and you deserve to close yourself off in some stuffy office in Dallas!" She swiped at the tear that trickled down her cheek, even more annoyed at herself for crying.

To her absolute consternation, Colby stood there smiling at her.

She thought she might slug him.

He kissed her before she could make up her mind.

And then she really did start crying.

"Oh, sugar. No. Don't cry." He brushed his thumbs beneath her eyes.

"Colby, I thought I could do this, but I just can't anymore. I want strings attached between us. Really, really strong ones—"

"So do I."

"And I know I said… What did you just say?"

"I said, I want those strings, too. I love you, Becca Sue. I never stopped loving you. I don't need some partnership in a big-city law firm. Who the hell am I trying to impress, anyway? My parents? They don't give a damn. I haven't even see them in twenty years. I'm happy in my private practice here in Hope Valley. I've got money and success…and the love of my life standing right in front of me. I don't need anything more."

"Oh, Colby, are you sure?" Even as she said the words, she knew they were dumb. Of course he was sure. She could see it in his eyes, feel it in his touch, his kiss.

"Sugar pie, if the drama in your life lately is any indication, I figure you're bound to need legal representation sometime in the future. And I'm your man. If you'll have me, I want to be your man forever."

"That's good because…" She pulled the stick from the pocket of her capris and glanced down at it.

She screamed and leaped into Colby's arms,

wrapping her legs around his waist, her arms around his neck.

"We're going to have a baby!"

He was speechless for a moment. "No kidding?"

"No kidding."

He kissed her. "Guess it's a good thing I didn't sell the farmhouse. Looks like we'll be putting more of those rooms to good use."

"Rooms, plural?" she asked.

"Yeah. You liked having brothers. I always hated being an only child. Seems we should make sure this baby has siblings to grow up with."

"Mmm. Three or four at least," she said.

"Man. I'll have to add onto the house."

She smiled. "We have time."

"Yes. All our lives. I love you, Becca Sue. I wish I hadn't been so stupid before—"

She put a finger over his lips. "We were awfully young then, Colby. Besides, now you're a full-fledged lawyer and can afford to keep me in the style to which I'd like to become accustomed."

He laughed, long and hard. This woman was the least money-hungry person he'd ever met.

"Well," he said. "I've already given up the lease on my office across the street. I suppose we could get your place spruced up, scour the antique sales for a bunch of junk to put back in it—"

"I don't sell junk."

"And we could turn the apartment into my office." He kissed the tip of her nose. "Sorry. *Merchandise,*" he corrected. "One rule, though."

"What's that?"

"No more overtime for either of us. We go home together at the end of each day. For the rest of our living days."

"Colby Flynn, that's an offer too tempting to refuse. I accept."

She sank into his kiss, right there in broad daylight on Main Street, and thought dreamily of the lifetime of temptations this sexy Texan would present.

* * * * *

"Now that's the kind of man you should be looking
for," my mother, the self-appointed keeper of my
shelf-life stamp, says. She points with her fork at a
man in the corner of the Steak-Out Restaurant, a
dive I've just been hired to redecorate. Making this
restaurant look four-star will be hard, but not half as
hard as getting through lunch without strangling the
woman across the table from me. "*He* would make
a good husband."

"Oh, you can tell that from across the room?" I
ask, wondering how it is she can forget that when

we had trouble getting rid of my last husband, she shot him. "Besides being ten minutes away from death if he actually eats all that steak, he's twenty years too old for me and—shallow woman that I am—twenty pounds too heavy. Besides, I am *so* not looking for another husband here. I'm looking to design a new image for this place, looking for some sense of ambience, some feeling, something I can build a proposal on for them."

My mother studies the man in the corner, tilting her head, the better to gauge his age, I suppose. I think she's grimacing, but with all the Botox and Restylane injected into that face, it's hard to tell. She takes another bite of her steak salad, chews slowly so that I don't miss the fact that the steak is a poor cut and tougher than it should be. "You're concentrating on the wrong kind of proposal," she says finally. "Just look at this place, Teddi. It's a dive. There are hardly any other diners. What does *that* tell you about the food?"

"That they cater to a dinner crowd and it's lunchtime," I tell her.

I don't know what I was thinking bringing her here with me. I suppose I thought it would be better than eating alone. There really are days when my common sense goes on vacation. Clearly, this is one of them. I mean, really, did I not resolve less than three weeks ago that I would not let my mother get to me anymore?

What good are New Year's resolutions, anyway?

Mario approaches the man's table and my mother studies him while they converse. Eventually Mario leaves the table with a huff, after which the diner glances up and meets my mother's gaze. I think she's smiling at him. That or she's got indigestion. They size each other up.

I concentrate on making sketches in my notebook and try to ignore the fact that my mother is flirting. At nearly seventy, she's developed an unhealthy interest in members of the opposite sex to whom she isn't married.

According to my father, who has broken the TMI rule and given me Too Much Information, she has no interest in sex with him. Better, I suppose, to be clued in on what they aren't doing in the bedroom than have to hear what they might be doing.

"He's not so old," my mother says, noticing that I have barely touched the Chinese chicken salad she warned me not to get. "He's got about as many years on you as you have on your little cop friend."

She does this to make me crazy. I know it, but it works all the same. "Drew Scoones is not my little 'friend.' He's a detective with whom I—"

"Screwed around," my mother says. I must look shocked, because my mother laughs at me and asks if I think she doesn't know the "lingo."

What I thought she didn't know was that Drew and I actually tangled in the sheets. And, since it's possible she's just fishing, I sidestep the issue and tell her that Drew is just a couple of years younger than me and that I don't need reminding. I dig into my salad with renewed vigor, determined to show my mother that Chinese chicken salad in a steak place was not the stupid choice it's proving to be.

After a few more minutes of my picking at the wilted leaves on my plate, the man my mother has me nearly engaged to pays his bill and heads past us toward the back of the restaurant. I watch my mother take in his shoes, his suit and the diamond pinkie ring that seems to be cutting off the circulation in his little finger.

"Such nice hands," she says after the man is out of sight. "Manicured." She and I both stare at my hands. I have two popped acrylics that are being held on at weird angles by bandages. My cuticles are ragged and there's marker decorating my right hand from measuring carelessly when I did a drawing for a customer.

Twenty minutes later she's disappointed that he managed to leave the restaurant without our noticing. He will join the list of the ones I let get away. I will hear about him twenty years from now when—according to my mother—my children will be grown and I will still be single, living pathetically alone with several dogs and cats.

After my ex, that sounds good to me.

The waitress tells us that our meal has been taken care of by the management and, after thanking Mario, the owner, complimenting him on the wonderful meal and assuring him that once I have redecorated his place people will be flocking here in droves (I actually use those words and ignore my mother when she rolls her eyes), my mother and I head for the restroom.

My father—unfortunately not with us today—has the patience of a saint. He got it over the years of living with my mother. She, perhaps as a result, figures he has the patience for both of them, and feels justified having none. For her, no rules apply, and a little thing like a picture of a man on the door to a public restroom is certainly no barrier to using the john. In all fairness, it does seem silly to stand and wait for the ladies' room if no one is using the men's room.

Still, it's the idea that rules don't apply to her, signs don't apply to her, conventions don't apply to her. She knocks on the door to the men's room. When no one answers she gestures to me to go in ahead. I tell her that I can certainly wait for the ladies' room to be free and she shrugs and goes in herself.

Not a minute later there is a bloodcurdling scream from behind the men's room door.

"Mom!" I yell. "Are you all right?"

Mario comes running over, the waitress on his heels. Two customers head our way while my mother continues to scream.

I try the door, but it is locked. I yell for her to open it and she fumbles with the knob. When she finally manages to unlock and open it, she is white behind her two streaks of blush, but she is on her feet and appears shaken but not stirred.

"What happened?" I ask her. So do Mario and the waitress and the few customers who have migrated to the back of the place.

She points toward the bathroom and I go in, thinking it serves her right for using the men's room. But I see nothing amiss.

She gestures toward the stall, and, like any self-respecting and suspicious woman, I poke the door open with one finger, expecting the worst.

What I find is worse than the worst.

The husband my mother picked out for me is sitting on the toilet. His pants are puddled around his ankles, his hands are hanging at his sides. Pinned to his chest is some sort of Health Department certificate.

Oh, and there is a large, round, bloodless bullet hole between his eyes.

Four Nassau County police officers are securing the area, waiting for the detectives and crime scene personnel to show up. They are trying, though not very hard, to comfort my mother, who in another era would be considered to be suffering from the vapors. Less tactful in the twenty-first century, I'd say she was losing it. That is, if I didn't know her better, know she was milking it for everything it was worth.

My mother loves attention. As it begins to flag, she swoons and claims to feel faint. Despite four No Smoking signs, my mother insists it's all right for her to light up because, after all, she's in shock. Not to mention that signs, as we know, don't apply to her.

When asked not to smoke, she collapses mournfully in a chair and lets her head loll to the side, all without mussing her hair.

Eventually, the detectives show up to find the four patrolmen all circled around her, debating whether to administer CPR, smelling salts or simply call the paramedics. I, however, know just what will snap her to attention.

"Detective Scoones," I say loudly. My mother parts the sea of cops.

"We have to stop meeting like this," he says lightly to me, but I can feel him checking me over with his eyes, making sure I'm all right while pretending not to care.

"What have you got in those pants?" my mother asks him, coming to her feet and staring at his crotch accusingly. *"Bayday?* Everywhere we Bayers are, you turn up. You don't expect me to buy that this is a coincidence, I hope."

Drew tells my mother that it's nice to see her, too, and asks if it's his fault that her daughter seems to attract disasters.

Charming to be made to feel like the bearer of a plague.

He asks how I am.

"Just peachy," I tell him. "I seem to be making a habit of finding dead bodies, my mother is driving me crazy and the catering hall I booked two freakin' years ago for Dana's bat mitzvah has just been shut down by the Board of Health!"

"Glad to see your luck's finally changing," he says, giving me a quick squeeze around the shoulders before turning his attention to the patrolmen, asking what they've got, whether they've taken any statements, moved anything, all the sort of stuff you see on TV, without any of the drama. That is, if you don't count my mother's threats to faint every few minutes when she senses no one's paying attention to her.

Mario tells his waitstaff to bring everyone espresso, which I decline because I'm wired enough. Drew pulls him aside and a minute later I'm handed a cup of coffee that smells divinely of Kahlúa.

The man knows me well. Too well.

His partner, whom I've met once or twice, says he'll interview the kitchen staff. Drew asks Mario if he minds if he takes statements from the patrons first and gets to him and the waitstaff afterward.

"No, no," Mario tells him. "Do the patrons first." Drew raises his eyebrow at me like he wants to know if I get the double entendre. I try to look bored.

"What is it with you and murder victims?" he asks me when we sit down at a table in the corner.

I search them out so that I can see you again, I almost say, but I'm afraid it will sound desperate instead of sarcastic.

My mother, lighting up and daring him with a look to tell her not to, reminds him that *she* was the one to find the body.

Drew asks what happened *this time*. My mother tells him how the man in the john was "taken" with me, couldn't take his eyes off me and blatantly flirted with both of us. To his credit, Drew doesn't laugh, but his smirk is undeniable to the trained eye. And I've had my eye trained on him for nearly a year now.

"While he was noticing you," he asks me, "did *you* notice anything about him? Was he waiting for anyone? Watching for anything?"

I tell him that he didn't appear to be waiting or watching. That he made no phone calls, was fairly intent on eating and did, indeed, flirt with my mother. This last bit Drew takes with a grain of salt, which was the way it was intended.

"And he had a short conversation with Mario," I tell him. "I think he might have been unhappy with the food, though he didn't send it back."

Drew asks what makes me think he was dissatisfied, and I tell him that the discussion seemed acrimonious and that Mario looked distressed when he left the table. Drew makes a note and says he'll look into it and asks about anyone else in the restaurant. Did I see anyone who didn't seem to belong, anyone who was watching the victim, anyone looking suspicious?

"Besides my mother?" I ask him, and Mom huffs and blows her cigarette smoke in my direction.

I tell him that there were several deliveries, the kitchen staff going in and out the back door to grab a smoke. He stops me and asks what I was doing checking out the back door of the restaurant.

Proudly—because, while he was off forgetting me, dropping by only once in a while to say hi to Jesse, my son, or drop something by for one of my daughters that he thought they might like, I was getting on with my life—I tell him that I'm decorating the place.

He looks genuinely impressed. "Commercial customers? That's great," he says. Okay, that's what he *ought* to say. What he actually says is "Whatever pays the bills."

"Howard Rosen, the famous restaurant critic, got her the job," my mother says. "You met him—the good-looking, distinguished gentleman with the *real* job, something to be proud of. I guess you've never read his reviews in *Newsday*."

Drew, without missing a beat, tells her that Howard's reviews are on the top of his list, as soon as he learns how to read.

"I only meant—" my mother starts, but both of us assure her that we know just what she meant.

"So," Drew says. "Deliveries?"

I tell him that Mario would know better than I, but that I saw vegetables come in, maybe fish and linens.

"This is the second restaurant job Howard's got her," my mother tells Drew.

"At least she's getting *something* out of the relationship," he says.

"If he were here," my mother says, ignoring the insinuation, "he'd be comforting her instead of interrogating her. He'd be making sure we're both all right after such an ordeal."

"I'm sure he would," Drew agrees, then looks me in the eyes as if he's measuring my tolerance for shock. Quietly he adds, "But then maybe he doesn't know just what strong stuff your daughter's made of."

It's the closest thing to a tender moment I can expect from Drew Scoones. My mother breaks the spell. "She gets that from me," she says.

Both Drew and I take a minute, probably to pray that's all I inherited from her.

"I'm just trying to save you some time and effort," my mother tells him. "My money's on Howard."

Drew withers her with a look and mutters something that sounds suspiciously like "fool's gold." Then he excuses himself to go back to work.

I catch his sleeve and ask if it's all right for us to leave. He says sure, he knows where we live. I say goodbye to Mario. I assure him that I will have some sketches for him in a few days, all the while hoping that this murder doesn't cancel his redecorating plans. I need the money desperately, the alternative being borrowing from my parents and being strangled by the strings.

My mother is strangely quiet all the way to her house. She doesn't tell me what a loser Drew Scoones is—despite his good looks—and how I was obviously drooling over him. She doesn't ask me where Howard is taking me tonight or warn me not to tell my father about what happened because he will worry about us both and no doubt insist we see our respective psychiatrists.

She fidgets nervously, opening and closing her purse over and over again.

"You okay?" I ask her. After all, she's just found a dead man on the toilet, and tough as she is that's got to be upsetting.

When she doesn't answer me I pull over to the side of the road.

"Mom?" She refuses to meet my eyes. "You want me to take you to see Dr. Cohen?"

She looks out the window as if she's just realized we're on Broadway in Woodmere. "Aren't we near Marvin's Jewelers?" she asks, pulling something out of her purse.

"What have you got, Mother?" I ask, prying open her fingers to find the murdered man's ring.

"It was on the sink," she says in answer to my dropped jaw. "I was going to get his name and address and have you return it to him so that he could ask you out. I thought it was a sign that the two of you were meant to be together."

"He's dead, Mom. You understand that, right?" I ask. You never can tell when my mother is fine and when she's in la-la land.

"Well, I didn't know that," she shouts at me. "Not at the time."

I ask why she didn't give it to Drew, realize that she wouldn't give Drew the time in a clock shop and add, "...or one of the other policemen?"

"For heaven's sake," she tells me. "The man is dead, Teddi, and I took his ring. How would that look?"

Before I can tell her it looks just the way it is, she pulls out a cigarette and threatens to light it.

"I mean, really," she says, shaking her head like it's my brains that are loose. "What does he need with it now?"

Silhouette®

nocturne™

**WAS HE HER SAVIOR
OR HER NIGHTMARE?**

HAUNTED
LISA CHILDS

Years ago, Ariel and her sisters were separated for
their own protection. Now the man who vowed
revenge on her family has resumed the hunt, and
Ariel must warn her sisters before it's too late.
The closer she comes to finding them, the more
secretive her fiancé becomes. Can she trust the man
she plans to spend eternity with? Or has he been
waiting for the perfect moment to destroy her?

On sale December 2006.

SNHDEC

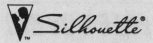

REQUEST YOUR FREE BOOKS!
2 FREE NOVELS PLUS 2
FREE GIFTS!

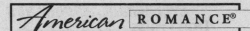

American **ROMANCE**®

Heart, Home & Happiness!

YES! Please send me 2 FREE Harlequin American Romance® novels and my 2 FREE gifts. After receiving them, if I don't wish to receive any more books, I can return the shipping statement marked "cancel." If I don't cancel, I will receive 4 brand-new novels every month and be billed just $4.24 per book in the U.S., or $4.99 per book in Canada, plus 25¢ shipping and handling per book and applicable taxes, if any*. That's a savings of close to 15% off the cover price! I understand that accepting the 2 free books and gifts places me under no obligation to buy anything. I can always return a shipment and cancel at any time. Even if I never buy another book from Harlequin, the two free books and gifts are mine to keep forever.

154 HDN EEZK 354 HDN EEZV

Name	(PLEASE PRINT)	
Address		Apt. #
City	State/Prov.	Zip/Postal Code

Signature (if under 18, a parent or guardian must sign)

Mail to the Harlequin Reader Service®:

IN U.S.A.	**IN CANADA**
P.O. Box 1867	P.O. Box 609
Buffalo, NY	Fort Erie, Ontario
14240-1867	L2A 5X3

Not valid to current Harlequin American Romance subscribers.

Want to try two free books from another line?
Call 1-800-873-8635 or visit www.morefreebooks.com.

* Terms and prices subject to change without notice. NY residents add applicable sales tax. Canadian residents will be charged applicable provincial taxes and GST. This offer is limited to one order per household. All orders subject to approval. Credit or debit balances in a customer's account(s) may be offset by any other outstanding balance owed by or to the customer. Please allow 4 to 6 weeks for delivery.

HAR06

Silhouette®
Desire

Don't miss

DAKOTA FORTUNES,

**a six-book continuing series following
the Fortune family of South Dakota—
oil is in their blood and privilege
is their birthright.**

This series kicks off with
USA TODAY bestselling author

PEGGY MORELAND'S
Merger of Fortunes
(SD #1771)

this January.

Other books in the series:

BACK IN FORTUNE'S BED by Bronwyn James (Feb)
FORTUNE'S VENGEFUL GROOM by Charlene Sands (March)
MISTRESS OF FORTUNE by Kathie DeNosky (April)
EXPECTING A FORTUNE by Jan Colley (May)
FORTUNE'S FORBIDDEN WOMAN by Heidi Betts (June)

In February, expect MORE from

HARLEQUIN® Romance®

as it increases to six titles per month.

What's to come...

Rancher and Protector

Part of the

Western Weddings
miniseries

BY JUDY CHRISTENBERRY

The Boss's Pregnancy Proposal

BY RAYE MORGAN

Don't miss February's
incredible line up of authors!